IMOGENE AND THE CASE

OF THE MISSING PEARLS

By

Elizabeth Varadan

Paperback ISBN 978-1-78092-758-9
ePub ISBN 978-1-78092-759-6
PDF ISBN 978-1-78092-760-2

Published in the UK by MX Publishing
335 Princess Park Manor, Royal Drive,
London, N11 3GX www.mxpublishing.co.uk
Cover design by www.staunch.com

Grateful acknowledgment to Conan Doyle Estate Ltd. for the use of the Sherlock Holmes characters created by Sir Arthur Conan Doyle.

For my husband, Rajan

Contents

Chapter One - Imogene Decides to Become a Detective

"Oh, do stop pacing," Imogene told her snooty older cousin, Sarah Jane. "The carriage will be ready soon." She drummed her fingers against the window seat thinking, but not soon enough!

"Imogene," said Miss Mullin, Imogene's governess, "A hostess never speaks sharply to guests."

They were in the schoolroom. Tea was over, but Miss Mullin remained at the small round dining table in one corner reading *The Daily Telegraph*.

Perry, Sarah Jane's younger brother, sat cross-legged on the floor a few feet away trying to make his lead soldiers

1

attack Twinkle, Imogene's cat who cowered under a chair. With a final, pitiful meow, Twinkle ran out of the room.

"Now look what you've done!" Imogene said.

They weren't even her real cousins. Uncle Hugh had married their mother last year, a widow Imogene had to call Aunt, and now Imogene was stuck with Sarah Jane and Perry who weren't the least bit friendly.

Sarah Jane strolled back and forth from one end of the long bookcase to the other. Each time she turned, her ankle-length skirt twirled against the white leather-button boots she'd been showing off all weekend. Imogene, who was ten-and-a-half, still wore shorter skirts.

"Don't you have any interesting books?" Sarah Jane asked. "These are all so childish." She held up a slim book and snickered. "*Goody Two Shoes*!"

Miss Mullin looked up again from her paper, her mouth puckered as if she'd just eaten a sour quince. "I chose that book," she said in her thin, raspy voice. "A fine book, with many good moral lessons in rhyme."

Imogene rolled her eyes. She'd had to memorize some of those rhymes and recite them for her parents, too.

But Sarah Jane put the book back in place and continued her strolling, not at all chastened. She pulled out another book and tittered. "*Black Beauty*! I remember that.

Told by a horse. As if a dumb animal could tell his life story! A nice little children's book, I suppose."

Imogene pressed her lips together to keep from saying something rude. She'd read *Black Beauty* at least four times and had cried many times over it. "Horses suffer a lot," she finally said. "People shouldn't whip them."

Perry looked up from his soldiers. "You have to whip them or they won't obey."

"When I'm older, I'm going be a horse doctor and take care of horses that have been treated badly."

"A highly unsuitable goal for a young lady!" said Miss Mullin.

"Florence Nightingale of the horses," Sarah Jane said. "How sweet." She laid the book on the shelf, wandered over to the table and flopped down opposite Miss Mullin.

"If you're so grown-up," Imogene told Sarah Jane crossly, "Why don't you read newspapers instead of going through my bookshelf?"

"I do read newspapers."

"Also highly unsuitable for a young lady," Miss Mullin said. "Except for the society section, of course."

Sarah Jane leaned forward to peer at the back page. "Oh. It looks like they're close to solving the case!" She leaned closer. "Rumor has it that Sherlock Holmes has been consulted," she read aloud. "Hmm."

Imogene got up from the window seat and came to peer over Sarah Jane's shoulder. She often peeked in *The Daily Telegraph* after it had been discarded by the adults, and she'd been following this case. Some diamond earrings and a necklace had been stolen from a mansion in Belgravia two weeks ago.

"Well, Sherlock Holmes will solve it," Sarah Jane said. "They say he doesn't look like much—tall and ever so skinny, but he's supposed to be frightfully smart."

"Yes, criminals are afraid of him," Imogene said. "But he should probably check the downpipe from the water closet. A clever thief could have gotten in that way."

"Imogene! A proper lady never mentions a water closet!"

Sarah Jane gave a scornful laugh. "What's this? Florence Nightingale of the horses knows what Sherlock Holmes needs to do? I suppose you're planning to be a detective now, instead of a vet.

Imogene jutted her chin. "I might just do."

Miss Mullin sighed loudly and crackled the newspaper, as if to say, Do be quiet!

"We're planning to move to Belgravia, you know," Sarah Jane said airily.

"Belgravia!" Miss Mullin lowered the newspaper, her eyes bugging out. "That's one of the richest neighborhoods in London!"

Sarah Jane smiled smugly. "That's why we're moving there."

The governess opened and closed her mouth. After a pause, she said, "You shouldn't be discussing your personal finances."

"I wasn't," Sarah Jane said, shrugging. "I just said we're moving to Belgravia."

Imogene waited for Miss Mullin to reprimand Sarah Jane for impertinence. Instead the governess folded her newspaper and rose.

"I feel a headache coming on," she said. "I've got to go lie down for a while."

As soon as Imogene could be sure Miss Mullin was out of earshot, she said, "Uncle Hugh can't afford Belgravia."

Sarah Jane gave a disdainful wave of the hand. "My mother says a smart solicitor should be able to afford a great deal. She says all he needs to do is push himself a little more, and if she had known he wasn't going to, she might not even have—"

"Uncle Hugh *is* smart," Imogene said angrily. "Father says your mother is ruining Uncle Hugh because all she thinks about is money." Uncle Hugh's anxious face rose in her mind. Before his marriage he had been so jovial and fun. Now whenever he visited, he was silent and mopey.

Sarah Jane rose, one hand on her hip. "Perry has boarding school to think of, and in two more years I'll be going to balls. If my mother didn't push your precious uncle, he'd be satisfied with living in Staines forever."

"What's wrong with Staines?" Imogene asked.

"Nothing, if you don't mind living near a stinky linoleum factory. All the important people live in Belgravia. But then, you wouldn't appreciate the importance of living in Belgravia. My mother says your mother is the daughter of a tailor and common."

Imogene caught her breath. "All the nice people live here in Kensington. And Staines will be a much nicer place once you move out!" She was pleased to see two red spots appear on Sarah Jane's cheeks, although that reaction didn't seem half enough after Sarah Jane's horrid comment.

"I wouldn't want to live in Belgravia," she added. "They rob houses in Belgravia."

Sarah Jane just laughed. "If they rob ours," she said, "we'll call you instead of Sherlock Holmes."

Imogene glared. That did it. She definitely would become a detective someday. And she would never solve any case for Sarah Jane or her mother.

Sarah Jane turned to her brother. "Perry, pick up your soldiers. We're going downstairs."

"But . . ."

"Perry!"

Perry reluctantly put his soldiers in the leather bag lying to one side and got to his feet, brushing off his black velvet Fauntleroy suit. Imogene watched him follow his sister as she flounced out the door, her bustle waving slightly with each step. The two of them nearly ran into Dottie the housemaid who stepped aside just in time.

Smoothing her white apron, Dottie said, "Miss Imogene, your mother says to come down and make your goodbyes; the carriage has come round." She peered over her shoulder to make sure the cousins weren't still lingering at the doorway and added in a whisper, "About time, too, only you din't hear me say that."

When Imogene didn't return her grin, the maid's normally pert face pinched up with concern. "Here, now, whatever that wicked girl said to cause such a look on your face, you just put right out of your mind. She likes to stir things up. I've heard her with her parents. She don't need to stir you up, too."

"Thank you, Dottie." Arms at her sides, Imogene took a deep breath and marched out to the landing.

Mr. Devon, the butler, was helping Uncle Hugh into his brown tweed frock coat and giving him his hat as Imogene came down the stairs. Aunt Letitia and Sarah Jane were already cloaked in their matching lace-trimmed capes, Perry standing beside his mother in his Fauntleroy suit, his hair still in ringlets.

Talk about childish, Imogene thought, as she joined them.

Mr. Devon ushered them to the door, and they all walked to the gate.

Mother and Aunt Letitia kissed each other's cheeks.

"You must come visit us soon," said Aunt Letitia in a voice as phony as her smile.

"Indeed," Mother said, her own voice cheery, as the coachman helped Aunt Letitia into the carriage. "Have a safe journey home." She patted Perry's shoulder as he scrambled in after his mother.

Imogene felt a yank of sympathy for the two handsome chestnut horses harnessed to the carriage. After Perry's remark in the schoolroom, she was sure the coachman would whip the horses on their long journey to Staines.

Father and Uncle Hugh shook hands. Uncle Hugh said, "Old Chap," and Father nodded stiffly, then put his hands behind his back, waiting while Uncle Hugh got in.

The coachman helped Sarah Jane into the carriage and folded up the step. And then they were off, the carriage rattling down the street.

When it rounded the corner, Mother gave a great sigh and said, "That's over for a while. Let's go back inside."

"Over for a good while this time, I think," Father said. He pursed his lips. "Hugh will probably go on a long sulk now that I've made it clear—"

Mother put a finger to her lips. Both parents glanced at Imogene. It was clear they didn't want her to hear Uncle Hugh's reason for a long sulk.

Her mother put an arm around Imogene as they went up the front steps and said, "You must be worn out, pet, after playing hostess to your cousins all weekend. I imagine you'd like to go upstairs and rest."

"I'm not a bit tired," Imogene said. In fact she felt positively lively now that the horrible cousins were gone.

"Well, your father and I could use a rest," her mother said. She gave a rueful little laugh.

"Let's go into the drawing room," her father murmured.

"Yes, I'll ring for tea."

So that was that. No hope of hearing about Uncle Hugh. Imogene decided to go find Twinkle and calm the poor cat down. A thorough search upstairs under the beds was probably a good place to begin.

"Beastly Perry," she muttered under her breath, since the word was unsuitable for young ladies and someone might hear. But when she reached the landing, a rapid click of footsteps in the hallway of her parents' wing made her peer around the corner.

Elsie, the new scullery maid, was hurrying toward the servants' stairs at the end of the hall. On a Sunday afternoon. How odd. Elsie was only supposed to be on this floor in the morning.

"Elsie," Imogene called. The maid stopped and turned, her eyes wide with fright.

"Oh! Miss Imogene! You startled me so!"

Imogene approached her. "I didn't mean to. But what are you doing upstairs at this time of day?"

"Oh, miss." The scullery maid lowered her eyes and fidgeted with a dusting cloth in her hand as Imogene came closer. "Dottie told me to clean the bathroom and water closet. But everyone were in and out whenever I come up to scrub. If it weren't yer auntie at breakfast, it were the little boy, and then it were the girl. I could never find a minute 'til now."

Elsie rattled off her explanation non-stop in such a quavering voice that Imogene felt sorry for her. Then she noticed Elsie only held the cloth, passing it from hand to hand. Now that she planned to be a detective, it was probably a good idea to notice details like that.

"Where's your pail and brush?" she asked.

"Please, miss." Elsie twisted the cloth in a frenzy. "I were done with scrubbing. I took the pail downstairs, but I remembered I left my rag upstairs. I dusts before I scrubs," she explained. "So I come to get it. The rag, I mean."

"Oh. Yes. I see," Imogene said slowly. But the timing still seemed strange.

"Please, miss, may I go?"

"Yes, of course."

Elsie gave a nervous curtsy, fleeing down the hall and out the door to the servants' stairs.

Imogene stared after her a moment. She supposed what Elsie said made sense. The maid could hardly clean the bathing room or water closet when someone was using them. Still, Elsie had acted so . . . guilty.

The weekend's unpleasantness floated through Imogene's mind in horrid little pictures—Sarah Jane's scornful face, Miss Mullin's sour-quince expression, her parents' secretive exchange of glances about Uncle Hugh. All because she was only ten. Almost eleven, really. Imogene put her hands on her hips, frowning in thought. There must something she could do to prove to them she wasn't just a child anymore.

But the next evening—Monday—brought a surprise that made Imogene's thoughts take a different turn. Her mother's pearls went missing.

Chapter Two - Theft in Kensington

Monday started off like any horrible Monday, with Miss Mullin praising the importance of beautiful handwriting. Today was the letter R. Imogene dipped her pen in her inkwell carefully, because if she made one splotch, she would have to start over.

"Why do I have to keep copying letters?" she grumbled. "It's not like I don't know my alphabet." Twinkle gave a small meow at Imogene's feet, as if agreeing. The cat had come out of hiding under Imogene's bed the night before, satisfied that tail-pulling Perry was gone.

Eyeing the cat distastefully, Miss Mullin said. "You must improve your script, Imogene! A lady's elegance is shown through her script. When you write invitations to parties later, people will judge you by it." With her long wooden pointer she tapped the slate blackboard on the wall where her own curly capital R headed a list of words and names beginning with loopy, slanted R's—words that would be part of a spelling test later.

And what good was Miss Mullin's elegant script? Imogene wondered, as she carefully scratched another R on the page with her pen. The governess was hardly writing invitations to parties now.

Next came the multiplication tables through twelves. More copy work—the only way to learn them, Miss Mullin claimed. But Imogene already knew up through her eights. Imogene suspected making her copy all of them was just to keep her busy, so the governess could think of other things.

Like now. Peeking up from her fifth 9 x 9, Imogene caught Miss Mullin studying a newspaper clipping.

As if she suddenly felt Imogene's gaze upon her, Miss Mullin looked up and quickly pocketed the scrap. "Carry on," she said.

For a brief time after lunch, Miss Mullin took a nap.

Imogene retrieved *Black Beauty* from the shelf where Sarah Jane had carelessly laid it and took it to her bedroom to read one more time. With Twinkle purring at her side, she melted once again into the world of Black Beauty's happy colt-hood on Squire Gordon's farm. She had just reached the sad part where the squire's son fell off his horse during the hunt, when Dottie tapped on her door.

"Excuse me, Miss Imogene, but Miss Mullin says it's time for your piano lesson."

With a sigh, Imogene closed the book and went down to the drawing room.

All through scales, Imogene thought about the book. It was such a moving story. So many people were cruel to their horses, not caring how they felt. And even the kind masters sometimes sold their horses to less kind owners. Like Squire Gordon did later when his wife became ill. Thinking about Black Beauty's coming miseries, Imogene missed F sharp.

"Where is your head today?" Miss Mullin demanded. "At this rate, you'll never play those pretty pieces your cousin played. And she played them so nicely!"

This time Imogene purposely missed both F sharp and, for good measure, G sharp.

At the end of the lesson, Miss Mullin claimed such poor playing had given her a headache and went to her room. The governess's headaches seemed to come on suddenly, and they lasted a good while. Pleased, Imogene returned to her room and the chance to read more of *Black Beauty* until her father came home from the bank and she could join her parents for family time.

Her thoughts kept skipping to the diamond theft in Belgravia. What exactly did detectives do? she wondered.

Where did they start? For one thing, they probably had to look around the house for footprints. For a while she pondered the merits of being a vet over the excitement of being a detective. Maybe her future cases would involve stolen horses.

Her thoughts were interrupted by Dottie's tap on the door. "Your mother and father are waiting."

Imogene hurried down to the drawing room.

Family time was their only time together, just the three of them. And Twinkle, of course, who always curled up in Imogene's lap.

Today Imogene's father lit his pipe and leaned back in his wing chair, a satisfied smile on his face. "I have a new client, with a sizable investment portfolio," he told her mother. "He breeds race horses at his stables in Surrey."

Horses! Imogene perked up.

"Have any of his horses raced at Epsom?" asked Mother.

"One of his horses came in third at the Epsom Derby a few years ago."

"It must be hard on the horses," Imogene said. "Racing, I mean."

Father laughed in a way that made both his dimples appear. "Not as hard as pulling a hansom cab or a carriage.

According to Atkins, the horses love racing. They get as excited as their jockeys."

Imogene sat back, reassured. "It's probably better than jumping hedges on a hunt," she said, thinking of the hunt at Squire Gordon's farm in *Black Beauty.*

Her mother smiled. "I had a nice day. I met a lady at a charity bazaar." With a sweet smile, she told Imogene, "I found out she has a daughter near your age. Perhaps I'll invite them both to tea."

Imogene tried to look pleased. Her mother sometimes took her to friends' teas in hopes Imogene and their daughters would become friends. Imogene always listened politely as the girls played piano or even recited poetry, but she found the whole thing dull.

"How would you like that, pet?"

"That would be . . ." What? Nice? Enjoyable? Imogene stroked Twinkle's ears, remembering Miss Mullin's claim that young ladies must be agreeable. "Interesting," she said.

"Lovely," Mother said. Her eyes lit with plans.

Imogene pressed her lips together. If this new girl came to tea, she certainly didn't intend to play scales or recite one of Miss Mullins's silly poems. She'd much prefer it if Mr. Atkins had a daughter her age, a daughter who would invite her to ride one of their horses.

"And how was your day, pet?"

Imogene wished her mother wouldn't call her "pet". It made her sound five years old. She picked through her day. "I'm still on multiplication," she said finally. "I know through nines, but this week I'm supposed to learn all through twelves."

Her father gave a nod of approval.

"And I'm working on my handwriting," she added. "Miss Mullin says a lady's character shows in her script."

Father waved his pipe in the air. "If you're good with numbers, it doesn't matter how pretty your letters are. Take me, for instance. Terrible handwriting, but that hasn't held me back." He raised his brows. "It's good enough for signing checks."

"I wish Pilkie could come back," Imogene suddenly blurted out. "Pilkie" was Nurse Pilkington, who had left a year ago to care for her sick mother.

"I know how you miss Pilkie," Mother said, and she gave a sympathetic cluck. "We all do. But even if she could come back, you're too old for a nursemaid. You need a governess to teach you music and elocution and such. I never had any of that at your age. "

"But you're fine without all that," Imogene said.

Her father burst into chuckles, his dimples reappearing. "She is," he agreed.

18

"You don't have to play piano or sing," Imogene pressed her point, "and everyone likes you just the way you are. I don't see why I have—" The disappointment on her mother's face stopped her.

"It's important for you to have these opportunities," Mother said quietly. "I want you to have all the advantages I never had."

As usual, family time ended too soon. At six o'clock, her parents went upstairs to change clothes for a dinner party.

Imogene was supposed to return to the nursery to eat with Miss Mullin, but she lingered a moment, fingering the locket her parents had given her on her last birthday. If only they would find a different governess for her! If only she could figure out how to let them know what a grump Miss Mullin was. But Miss Mullin was clever about speaking sweetly to Imogene when Mother or Father were present.

"I'll find a way," Imogene muttered to Twinkle. Cuddling the cat, she went out to the stairs.

At the top step, she heard excited voices from her parents' wing. She stepped quickly to the hall and saw Dottie rushing into Mother's room from the servant's door. Imogene set Twinkle down and hurried to her mother's doorway in time to hear Dottie say, "Oh, no, ma'am! How terrible, ma'am!"

"What happened?" Imogene asked.

Mother stood by the dresser, her face wet with tears, holding out an enameled jewel case to Father. The lid was open. The case was empty.

"Perhaps you mislaid them," Father was saying.

"I put them in this case on the dresser," Mother insisted. "Right after I came up from dinner Saturday night."

Seeing her mother's tears, Imogene almost felt like crying herself. Mother had been so cheerful and happy only a little while ago. "What happened?" she asked again, this time to Dottie.

"Her pearls are gone, miss," said the maid, her face wrung with worry.

"Oh!" Imogene put a hand to her mouth.

"I'm sure they'll turn up," Father said to Mother.

"Maybe they fell on the floor," Imogene said.

Dottie bent over to look under the dresser, then the night table.

"I've looked," Mother said. "I've looked everywhere. But I know I put them in their proper place."

"There's nowhere else you could have put them? A drawer?" Father asked.

"I would never just put them in the drawer." Mother wiped away her tears, "This is their special case. I always put them here."

Father rubbed his forehead, frowning. "Dottie, did you see anyone suspicious loitering around the house yesterday or today?"

The housemaid had stooped to peer under the wardrobe. She straightened up. "No, I din't, Mister Walters. I din't see no-one. But then, it's been ever so busy."

Mother dabbed her eyes with a handkerchief. "I'll wear my cameo tonight." She sniffled and added. "I suppose we'll have to report this to the police."

"No," Father said curtly. "Before you know it, it will be in *The Daily Telegraph* or *The Times*, with reporters everywhere. I'll send for a private detective, one who can be discreet." He went to the bell pull by the wardrobe and rang it. "I'll send for Sherlock Holmes."

Imogene's eyes widened. Sherlock Holmes!

Father wrote something on a notepad he took from his pocket. When the butler appeared, he said, "Devon, have Jonathan take this to Baker Street and wait for a reply." Jonathan was their groom, but he also doubled as their coachman.

"I suppose that's best," Mother said. "Mr. Holmes *is* rather famous for solving things." She closed the jewel case and set it on the dresser, her expression still mournful.

Father put his arm around her. "Mr. Holmes is the most brilliant detective in all of London. He'll find your pearls."

Imogene hoped so. She couldn't bear to see her mother so miserable.

Her conversation with Sarah Jane came vividly to mind. All the nice people are in Kensington, she'd told her snooty cousin. They rob houses in Belgravia. But somebody not very nice had just stolen Mother's pearls, right here in Kensington.

A sizzle of excitement followed Imogene's first sense of shock. Sherlock Holmes was coming to their house. Not only would he find the pearls, but she could watch how he went about solving his cases.

Chapter Three - Imogene Listens at the Door

"Must you fidget so!" scolded Miss Mullin, and Imogene stopped tapping her foot. The governess leaned over her huge square desk by the chalkboard as she thumbed through a book of poetry, searching for a suitable poem for Imogene to recite.

Imogene was supposed to be composing a poem of her own. Miss Mullin had suggested nature, but Imogene couldn't stop thinking about the stolen pearls. After a few words that rhymed with sky—pie, sigh, my—she found herself listing pearls . . . twirls. Theft . . . left. Her thoughts skipped to an idea that had been growing ever since she woke up this morning.

What if she were to find a clue that Mr. Holmes could use? What if she could help him find Mother's pearls? According to Dottie, Mr. Sherlock Holmes was supposed to arrive at ten o'clock, but the morning seemed to stretch on and on, as if the clock hands had stopped working properly.

At last the clip-clop of horses' hooves on the cobblestones outside, then the sound of a door clattering shut, announced the detective's arrival. Imogene jumped up and ran to the window. Two men had gotten out of a hansom cab. One was so tall and thin he made Imogene think of an exclamation point. He wore a dark morning coat and a tall hat. He tapped a furled umbrella against the pavement while saying something to his mustached companion, a shorter, wiry man wearing a bowler hat like Father's.

Imogene sensed Miss Mullin at her side. Remembering Sarah Jane's description, she told the governess, "The tall one is Sherlock Holmes."

"Humph," Miss Mullin said. "Neither one of them looks like a detective to me."

Imogene studied Mr. Holmes's long, thin face as he opened the wrought iron gate and approached the front steps. Was that a friendly or an unfriendly face? If she did find a clue, would she be able to talk to him?

"Oh, dear," Miss Mullin said with a sigh. Imogene turned. "I believe one of my headaches is coming on. I'll just go lie down for a while."

Imogene could hardly believe her luck. As soon as the governess left the schoolroom, one hand to her temple, Imogene counted to ten to give her time to go into her room. Then she tiptoed downstairs to the entrance hall in time to see

Mr. Devon, the butler, close the door behind the visitors. Twinkle followed at her side.

"I understand Mr. and Mrs. Walters wish to see me," said Mr. Holmes, as Mr. Devon took their hats.

Imogene's parents appeared in the hall.

Father said, "Don't you have lessons, Imogene? Your mother and I need to have a private discussion with Mr. Holmes."

"And with Dr. Watson," Mr. Holmes said. "You may tell him anything you would tell me."

"Let's go into the drawing room. I'll ring for tea," Mother said. "Or would you prefer coffee?"

"Coffee, thank you, if it isn't any trouble."

"Not at all," Mother said. She sent Imogene a glance.

Imogene started dutifully up the stairs, but Twinkle, curious as always, followed the visitors around the corner into the hall. As soon as Imogene felt sure they were all in the drawing room, she stole back down and tiptoed the doorframe to listen.

Mother was crying again. Her voice came out in little spurts. "They were . . . *sniff* . . . a wedding gift . . . *sniff* . . . from Mr. Walters."

"I see." Mr. Holmes said. "And when did you discover them missing?"

"Last evening, when we were getting ready to go out."

Imogene heard Father thump the arm of his wing-backed armchair. "Blast it! I don't see how anyone could have—"

"When was the last time you saw the pearls?"

"Saturday evening, at dinner," Father said, "when my brother and his new family were visiting."

Imogene peeped around the edge of the door for a quick glimpse of the detective. He sat at one end of the rose-colored sofa, leaning slightly forward, his fingertips tapping together. Dr. Watson was at the other end of the sofa, petting Twinkle, who had curled up beside him. Imogene quickly drew back, she hoped before anyone noticed.

"A social visit, Mr. Walters?" the detective asked.

Father's voice took on an edge. "Actually, Mr. Holmes, my brother was here to ask for a loan. Apparently he lost money again at his card club."

"Was this the first time he asked for money?"

After a pause, Father cleared his throat, coughed, and said, in that same edged voice, "No. But I did tell him it's the last."

"And did you loan him the money?"

"For once, I said no."

Imogene drew in a sharp breath. So that's why Uncle Hugh was going to have a long sulk!

"I see," Mr. Holmes said again. "I assume you close your windows at night?"

"Our butler assures me all the ground floor and basement windows were latched," Father said.

"No windows opened at all?"

"Only my wife's window, but it's too high for someone to get in. All the bedrooms are upstairs on the first floor."

"Do you have a large staff?"

"Not very large," said Father.

"A butler, a cook, a housemaid," said Mother. "And a scullery maid. And a governess. Then, of course, our groom who doubles as coachman."

"Dr. Watson and I are finishing up another case, so I fear I must wait until tomorrow to interview your staff."

"Interview our staff?" Mother sounded alarmed. "I doubt any of them would steal from us. They're devoted to us."

"They may have seen or heard something that could help us find the thief," Mr. Holmes explained.

"Oh, I see," said Mother. "We also have a jobbing gardener who comes on Mondays and Thursdays."

"We'll interview him Thursday, then. Before we leave, Dr. Watson will write down a list of your staff, their names and duties for our interviews tomorrow, and then with your permission, I should like to have a look around the first floor rooms and the outside premises."

"Certainly," Father said.

At that moment, Imogene couldn't resist another peek. This time she found the detective looking back at her with a piercing gaze that seemed to see her every thought. A slight smile pulled the corner of his mouth.

"You can come out from behind the doorway if you wish, Imogene," he said.

Her parents turned their heads in surprise as Imogene, flushing with embarrassment, came into the room.

"Imogene, why were you hiding?" her father asked.

"I wasn't hiding," Imogene said. She folded her hands to look ladylike. "I just didn't want to interrupt." She was pleased to see both their faces soften.

"That's sweet of you, pet," Mother said. She dabbed away her tears and smoothed a pale wisp of hair from her face. "What did you want?"

"I wanted Twinkle," Imogene said. The cat was sitting next to Dr. Watson, batting at the pen in the doctor's hand.

"She dotes on that cat," her mother told the visitors.

"I can see why," said Dr. Watson. "Playful little thing." His voice seemed to have hidden chuckles in it. He tucked his pen in a pocket and handed the cat to Imogene.

Since there was no reason to linger, Imogene dropped a curtsy and left the room, vexed with herself for taking that second peek.

Walking toward the entrance hall and stairs, she reminded herself Mr. Holmes and Dr. Watson were coming back the next day. But now that she couldn't eavesdrop, how would she be able learn more about the theft?

Imogene rubbed the cat's chin, mulling over what she'd learned so far—all the lower windows were latched; only her mother's window was open upstairs.

The first thing she must do is to go outside and look at the back wall to see how difficult it would be to climb through her mother's window.

Chapter Four - Suspects and Promises

"Those pearls had to be taken sometime during the night," Mrs. Parker said in a low voice. She wiped a crumb from her mouth. The stout cook had spied Imogene on her way out the back door and asked if she wanted a raspberry scone.

Mrs. Parker was a widow and had worked for the family for as long as Imogene could remember. She was also Imogene's trusted friend. And her raspberry scones were delicious. Imogene munched contentedly. She still planned to check her mother's window, but now it seemed wise to find out if Mrs. Parker had seen anything suspicious.

Mrs. Parker leaned forward and added, "An inside job, while everyone slept!"

"Mr. Holmes thinks so, too."

"Does he, now?"

"I think he does. He's coming tomorrow to interview everyone."

"At the door again, were you?"

"Until Mr. Holmes told on me."

"Dottie would have caught you."

"Dottie wouldn't have told."

"True," Mrs. Parker conceded. Imogene knew Mrs. Parker counted on Dottie's eavesdropping. A gleam came into the cook's grey eyes. "As for those pearls, I'll wager I know who did it!"

Imogene carefully swallowed her bite of scone, remembering how calm Mr. Holmes had seemed all through his interview with her parents. That was how a detective behaved.

"I see," she said. When she found the pearls, or at least helped Mr. Holmes find them, her parents would be sorry they sent her from the parlor, and Mr. Holmes would be impressed. "Who do you think took them?" she asked.

Mrs. Parker leaned closer and looked around. "Mr. Devon, that's who."

"Really!" Imogene blurted out, then reminded herself to stay calm.

"See for yourself. He left not fifteen minutes ago. Says he has an errand, but I'll wager he's out pawning those pearls this very minute."

Mr. Devon had been hired a month ago after the previous butler, Mr. Stewart, retired. Mr. Devon looked pretty old, too, in Imogene's opinion. He walked slowly and spoke slowly. Her mother said it showed how dignified he was. But Mr. Devon wouldn't even have to climb through a window to get to the pearls. He lived right here in the house. An inside job. Imogene pulled at one of her curls, thinking.

Mrs. Parker reached over with a smile and straightened Imogene's bow. "Blonde hair is so pretty. I hope your know-it-all governess has told you about rinsing with lemon juice. It brings out your highlights."

"She hasn't," said Imogene. It was comforting to know that Dottie and Mrs. Parker disliked the governess as much as she did.

"She'd do better to tend to her own job, than to complain of my puddings."

"Meow," said Twinkle, from the door where she stood, tail waving.

"Let her out, will you?" said Mrs. Parker. "Your legs are younger."

With a hurried thank you and a last bite of scone, Imogene picked Twinkle up and went out the kitchen door. She climbed the steps to the terrace and crossed to the rose trellis that opened onto the back garden. As she deposited Twinkle under the bush, she pondered Mrs. Parker's words. *Out selling the pearls this very minute.*

32

Imogene had thought Mr. Devon rather nice. Once he had told her she reminded him of his granddaughter. But she didn't really know him well. Mrs. Parker was usually right about things. Imogene pressed her lips together. Her thoughts were interrupted by voices as Mr. Holmes and Dr. Watson rounded the back corner of the house.

"They have a water closet, so someone may have climbed the downpipe," Mr. Holmes was saying. "I'm confident we shall solve this matter. Tonight I'll play my violin and think on it."

He halted. "Hullo, I see we have company."

Imogene gave the men a shy smile, her inner heart thrilling to what she had just heard. Sarah Jane may have scoffed at her comment about a downpipe, but here was Mr. Holmes talking about the very same thing!

"If I'm very quiet and don't disturb you," Imogene said, 'may I watch you work?"

Under his mustache, Dr. Watson's lips widened in a Cheshire cat smile.

"A budding detective!" Mr. Holmes said. "I don't see why not. Every pair of eyes helps on a case." He tapped his lower lip with his finger, squinting. Then he took a magnifying glass from his pocket and crossed the patio to the part of the ground that ran along the base of the wall and bent low. After a moment he pocketed the glass and studied the wall.

Imogene watched with interest.

Twinkle ran to Dr. Watson, who leaned over to scratch her head.

"Only one set of footprints and a single track mark," Mr. Holmes muttered. "A wheelbarrow, I suppose. No places in the bricks to serve as handholds . . ."

Imogene said, "What about the downpipe?"

He turned, the corners of his mouth twitching. "A good possibility."

"But I don't think anyone outside did it."

"And why is that?" asked the detective.

Now that she had his attention, Imogene chose her words carefully. "I may know who took the pearls."

The two men exchanged glances before Mr. Holmes strolled over to her, a pucker between his brows. "And who would that be?"

She took a deep breath, suddenly aware that Mr. Holmes was very tall and that he looked very serious. "Some people think it could have been . . . the butler. But actually," Imogene added quickly, "Mr. Devon is old. He might have trouble climbing the stairs."

34

A smile tugged at the corner of the detective's mouth. Dr. Watson cleared his throat and looked away.

"Perhaps I should notify the police to have him arrested," Mr. Holmes suggested.

Imogene blinked. "Arrested?"

"If he took the pearls."

"But I, um . . . I thought you were just making a list of suspects," Imogene stammered. "Mrs.—" She stopped. Somehow she was getting everyone in trouble.

The detective bent close. "Imogene," he said gently, "the butler never does it except in penny dreadfuls."

"Oh."

"You do know what penny dreadfuls are?"

Imogene nodded. "Dottie reads them. She says they're ever so exciting and romantic." When Mr. Holmes didn't say anything, Imogene added, "Father says they're not worth the paper they're printed on."

"Nevertheless," Mr. Holmes said, straightening, "everybody is under suspicion—including the butler, until evidence rules him out."

"Everybody?" Imogene frowned. That meant Mrs. Parker. And Dottie. Her friends.

"Everybody. And now, I'm afraid our business here is concluded for today. Shall we go, Watson?" He tipped his hat to Imogene. The two men started up the side path to the front. Imogene followed.

"Do you really think someone climbed up the downpipe?" she asked.

"I say, Holmes," said Dr. Watson, "she appears to be already working on this case. Maybe she could be our assistant."

Mr. Holmes turned to him. "You might have a point, Watson." He rubbed his chin. "Would you be interested?" he asked Imogene.

The very thing she had hoped for! Imogene smoothed the ruffles on her overskirt and said, in what she hoped was a calm and sensible voice, "Yes, I would, sir."

"You must keep your eyes and ears open and tell me everything you see."

She swallowed. "How will I do that, sir? Let you know, I mean."

Mr. Holmes tapped his chin. "Write down whatever clues you notice; then find a way to get a note to me."

"I could put it under the tray on the table in the entrance hall. That's where Dottie or Mr. Devon put Mother's invitations."

"How would I take a note from under the tray with no one noticing?"

Imogene thought hard. "What about the big pot with the geranium, inside the gate?"

The detective nodded. "I'll send a messenger tonight to check for your note."

"The gate squeaks sometimes," she warned.

"Yes, I noticed."

"But the gates to the carriage house don't squeak."

"The front gate will do," Mr. Holmes assured her. "It's a matter of oiling the hinges." He leaned close. "Don't tell anyone you are on this case, or you'll alert the suspect."

"Not anyone?"

"No one."

"Sometimes people have information they don't know is important," Dr. Watson explained. "You want everyone to feel they can talk to you freely."

"I understand," Imogene said, and she bit her lip. She was in the habit of telling Dottie and Mrs. Parker everything. "I won't say a word," she promised.

They were at the front patio by then. The detective looked her over, head to toe. "By the way, did you enjoy the scone you had before you left Twinkle beside the rosebush?"

Imogene gasped. "How did you . . ?"

"There's a bit of fresh dirt on the toe of your boot. Also, a rose petal is clinging to your cotton stocking, just above your boot top, along with two gray cat hairs. You must have brushed against the bush when you put Twinkle down. And the crumbs caught in the fold of your overskirt look to my expert eye like scone crumbs. Certainly not toast crumbs."

Dazzled, Imogene whispered, "It's all true."

"Good day." He gave her a nod and opened the gate for his companion. Dr. Watson tipped his bowler hat. Imogene watched them proceed up the street. A moment later, the detective hailed a hansom cab, and they climbed into the two-wheeled carriage that rumbled on its way, the horse hooves clopping loudly on the cobblestone street.

Imogene closed the gate carefully and went around to the back. Spying her cat stretched out under the rosebush, she said, "Twinkle, you would never believe how Mr. Holmes can figure out so much from crumbs and cat hairs and dirt on a boot."

To think that even such small clues could be so important!

I must be sure to look for clues like that, Imogene thought. Hoping for another scone, she went down the stairs to the kitchen.

Chapter Five – Imogene Makes a List

Legs dangling from her chair, Imogene asked the cook, "Why do you think Mr. Devon did it? Wouldn't it be silly of him to steal something when he's new on the job?" The rich aroma of roast duck floated from the oven. Mrs. Parker paused and turned from the vegetable soup she was stirring and eyed Imogene.

"Silly, is it?" She snapped her fingers. "This could be the last we'll see of him. For all you know, he's sold the pearls, changed his name, and is booking passage to Australia." She frowned and added, "You'd think he was a butler to royalty before coming here. Too superior to talk to the likes of me. Mr. Stewart was much friendlier. Such a pity he retired."

Imogene couldn't help noticing Mrs. Parker sounded eager to get Mr. Devon into trouble.

A soft "meow" seeped under the kitchen door.

"Let Twinkle in, will you?"

Imogene scooted off her chair and went to the door. She opened it and picked up the cat.

A thought made her pause. Why was Mrs. Parker so sure it was Mr. Devon? Was it because he wasn't friendly? Or had she seen him do something?

The cook sighed and tapped her ladle on the soup pot. "Well, I have to check on my duck and then think about tonight's pudding."

Imogene flashed her a smile, then wandered out of the kitchen, wrapped in her thoughts. It was time to make that list of clues for Mr. Holmes.

When she rounded the newel post at the top of the stairs, she tiptoed down the hall and peeked at Miss Mullin's door across from her own. Still closed. She hurried back to the schoolroom, put Twinkle in the cat's wicker basket bed, and went to her desk.

Lifting the top, Imogene sorted through papers, books, and copybooks and took out the diary her parents had given her last Christmas. She untied the blue ribbon wrapped around it and thumbed idly through the pages—descriptions of tea parties she'd gone to and disliked, a few remarks about Miss Mullin, a sketch of Twinkle, a complaint about the silliness of embroidering another sampler.

Boys get to do all the interesting things, she'd written. *If I weren't a girl, I could have my own stables and breed racehorses. Or I could be a horse doctor. Maybe I will be a horse doctor.* She had underlined "will".

Sunday she'd written about the diamonds that were stolen in Belgravia, adding, *I've decided to become a detective instead of a horse doctor.* All of a sudden she wondered if the diamond theft was the case Mr. Holmes said he was finishing up.

Which reminded Imogene of the list of clues Mr. Holmes wanted. She turned to a clean page.

Twinkle ran to Imogene and hopped into her lap. Imogene patted the cat's head absently, trying to think. Dipping her pen in the inkwell, she wrote: CLUES, then pursed her lips.

If the butler didn't do it, who could it be? Mrs. Parker's legs were too old to climb, and Dottie was always busy. What about Elsie? She had been upstairs Sunday, and at an odd time, too. Imogene wrote all this down.

Twinkle purred and reached up a paw to bat at Imogene's silver locket.

"Silly thing, it's not a toy," Imogene scolded. She repositioned the cat in her lap, thinking some more.

Was it Aunt Letitia? Father had just told Mr. Holmes that Uncle Hugh was asking for money. Aunt Letitia's room was right across from Mother's. She'd gone down late to breakfast. But Aunt Letitia always went late to breakfast when she visited. There was nothing unusual about that.

Then there were the horrible cousins. Perry would have no use for a necklace, but Sarah Jane could have poked through Mother's things when everyone was downstairs. Imogene felt a mean satisfaction at the idea. Sarah Jane a common thief!

No. Mother had the pearls Saturday evening. And on Sunday, when the cousins weren't at meals, they were either in Imogene's bedroom, with Perry making his lead soldiers attack her doll's house, or in the schoolroom, with Sarah Jane scoffing at Imogene's books.

For a moment Imogene let herself picture telling Sarah Jane how she helped Sherlock Holmes solve this case. "I've been too busy for childish things like piano . . ."

Piano. Imogene narrowed her eyes. What about Miss Mullin with her endless headaches? Miss Mullin's new headache came on the moment she saw Mr. Holmes and Dr. Watson coming up the walk. Monday, the governess had taken a nap after lunch and gone to bed again with a headache after the piano lesson. Or said she did. Imogene all wrote this down under number eight and underlined it. "I think we have our suspect," she told Twinkle.

The idea was cheering. She would like so much for thin, crabby Miss Mullin to be forced to leave.

If only Pilkie would come back!

Pilkie's real name was Susan Pilkington. But she had told Dottie and Mrs. Parker and Imogene to call her Pilkie, and the name had stuck. Only Imogene's parents ever called her Nurse Pilkington.

Pilkie used to take Imogene to the park and to the zoo. Sometimes they went to a tea shop and had milky tea and toasted muffins. Pilkie even taught Imogene to read. Then when she went home last year to take care of her sick mother, Imogene's parents hired Miss Mullin instead of a new nursemaid.

Imogene wrote a second copy of her suspicions in her diary's back page and tore out the first copy. This she folded into squares and put in her pocket. She placed the diary once more under her books and copybooks, then stood up, dumping Twinkle on the floor. The cat gave a meow of protest.

"Come along," Imogene said. "Once I put this note under the geranium pot, I'll make you a button on a string. You need a proper toy to play with."

Halfway down the stairs, she stopped. What if Miss Mullin read her diary? Imogene tried to think if anything ever looked different when she opened her desk. She couldn't remember.

"She'd never think to look on the last page, anyway," Imogene whispered to Twinkle. Remembering an earlier entry, she added, "And it's her fault if she reads that she's an old crab."

Imogene hurried down to the front door, intent on her mission.

Chapter Six – Imogene Meets Rusty

At nine o'clock the next morning, a boy with a threadbare cap and rumpled clothes came to the back door that lead to the kitchen. Imogene was eating poached eggs and sausage with Mrs. Parker. She was supposed to have breakfast with Miss Mullin every morning, but the governess had slept late again, which suited Imogene just fine. She much preferred eating with the cook.

Imogene stared at the boy. She doubted he was any older than she was. His wild ginger hair straggled below his ears and freckles covered his face. While she was noting this, he reached under his cap and pulled out a scrap of paper.

"What's this, then?" said Mrs. Parker, when he handed it to her.

"It's from Mr. 'Olmes for Mr. Walters," said the boy. "Says can 'e have a reply?"

Wait here," Mrs. Parker said, as she left the boy standing at the door and went upstairs to deliver the note.

As soon as she left the room, Imogene asked, "What's your name?"

The boy eyed the iron range where more sausages sizzled in a frying pan. He ran the tip of his tongue over his lower lip and swallowed. "They calls me Rusty."

Imogene smiled. "That suits you."

Rusty shrugged. He remained in the doorway, his eyes darting around the kitchen. His glance came to rest on Mrs. Parker's worktable where two loaves of bread were cooling.

The silence deepened between them.

"You don't say much, do you?" Imogene finally said.

"Ain't much to say."

"You could ask my name." When he didn't respond she said, "It's Imogene." He shrugged and she added, "I'm ten."

"I'm almost eleven."

"Well, that makes you ten, too," Imogene said with some annoyance. "Do you deliver many notes for Mr. Holmes?"

"I'm 'is main messenger."

Imogene felt a stab of jealousy. "I'm his assistant," she told him.

"Yeah. I took 'im yer note last night."

Imogene frowned. "I hope you didn't read it."

He shook his head. "But I does know how to read," he said after a pause.

"Did you read Mr. Holmes's note?" Imogene asked. When he shifted his gaze, she knew he had. "Can you tell me what was in it?"

"It's private, ain't it?"

"I'll ask the cook to give you something, if you tell me."

Rusty grinned. "'E's coming at ten to talk to all the servants, an' is that a good time?"

"All?" Imogene asked in dismay. It seemed clear that only Miss Mullin needed questioning. "Are you sure the note said *all?*"

At that moment Mrs. Parker bustled in with the slip of paper and gave it to Rusty.

"There's your reply for Mr. Holmes."

"Shouldn't he have something for his trouble?" asked Imogene.

The cook raised her eyebrows. "Why, yes, I suppose so." Reaching into the folds of her skirt beneath her apron, she pulled out a coin. "A halfpenny for your pains," she told him.

Imogene watched Rusty put the note and the coin under his cap. "Why don't you just put everything in your pocket?"

He looked down. "The bigger boys in the street sometimes ask me to empty me pockets."

Imogene was at a loss for words. Rusty was just turning to leave, when she thought to ask, "Have you eaten yet?"

He hesitated. "I ain't one for breakfast."

Mrs. Parker put her hands on her hips. "As scrawny as you are, you'd best have a bite." She went to her worktable and sliced a round of bread, wrapping it around two sausages. "There, that should do you."

Rusty flashed a smile at Imogene and sprinted away.

"Not one for thank yous is he?" the cook said. She cocked her head. "That was thoughtful of you, Imogene. I'll wager there's not much in his house to eat. For all we know, he could be an orphan."

Her manner grew brisk then. "I'd better get busy and grind some beans. They'll be here soon enough."

"Who?" asked Imogene, pretending ignorance.

"Who do you think sent that note?" Mrs. Parker asked with a wry look. "Dottie told me that Mr. Devon told her to look sharpish around ten. I imagine Mr. Holmes and the good doctor will be wanting a nice cup of coffee when they get here."

"Oh, you would make such a splendid detective," Imogene exclaimed.

What a shame she couldn't tell Mrs. Parker she was working on the case.

Chapter Seven - An Invitation

A few minutes later, Dottie hurried into the kitchen.

"Miss Imogene," she said, breathlessly, "The post just arrived. This came for you." She held out a small square envelope.

"For me?" Imogene said, pleased. Who it could be? She didn't get cards except from her grandparents on her birthday or Christmas.

"I couldn't help noticing it was from Staines," Dottie said.

"Couldn't help noticing?" said the cook with a wry look.

"Staines!" Imogene grimaced. "It's from Sarah Jane." For a moment she was tempted to throw it away.

Sure enough, the envelope was addressed in the kind of elegant, flowing script that Miss Mullin would have praised.

"You can use this to open it," Dottie prodded. She handed Imogene a sharp knife, the handle turned toward Imogene.

"Maybe some people like to read their mail in private," Mrs. Parker suggested, but Imogene could tell by the cook's lifted brows that she was just as curious.

Imogene took the knife from Dottie and slit the top of the envelope, while the cook and maid huddled next to her to read over her shoulder.

In splendid swirls and loops her cousin had written, "My Dear Cousin, Since you like Staines so much, you simply must visit us before we move." Both "like" and "must" had been underlined twice. "This weekend is the perfect time. Our coachman will meet you and Miss Mullin at the train station Saturday noon and you can return Monday morning. Perhaps we can visit the linoleum factory while you're here. I'm sure you would love that. Yours Ever So Affectionately, Sarah Jane."

"Ordering you around, it sounds like," said Dottie.

Mrs. Parker clucked her tongue.

Imogene crumpled the note and put it in her pocket. "I shan't go!" she told her friends. "She's just being nasty."

"That girl is meanness itself," Dottie said.

"And where do you think she gets it?" asked Mrs. Parker. She returned to the counter and measured out several spoonfuls of coffee beans from a jar into the coffee grinder. Then she rotated the coffee grinder handle with brisk, angry motions. "That mother of hers must have swallowed a wasp's nest. Never a kind word for anyone."

She stopped and wagged a finger at Imogene. "Your mother, now. She knows how to treat people."

"Where are they moving to?" Dottie asked.

"Belgravia." Imogene scowled.

"My, my!" The maid laughed. "Coming up in the world!"

But Imogene couldn't smile. Ladies had to respond to invitations. Mother would expect her to write back and accept.

"I'll have to go," she said.

Mrs. Parker pursed her lips and spoke to the coffee beans. "If you had a toothache, I don't imagine you could go."

"That girl *is* a toothache," Dottie said.

Imogene joined their giggling. Then Mrs. Parker's smile faded.

"No, I suppose you're right. It's probably best you go. Otherwise, they'll expect you to set a time when you can come. You might as well get it over with."

Imogene didn't answer.

Mrs. Parker walked over and put her arm around Imogene. "Here now," she said, squeezing Imogene's shoulder. "It's only for two days, and then you'll be home again."

Imogene nodded, dutifully, leaning against the cook's comforting bulk. It was going to be a horrid weekend.

"And I'll pack some nice tarts for you to have on the train," Mrs. Parker promised. "Now, why don't you go show your mother the invitation before Mr. Holmes gets here. She may still be in the breakfast room."

Imogene found her mother in the drawing room, standing by the window, next to the tall potted fern. She was wearing her plaid silk day dress and fingering a medallion at her neck, a faraway look on her face. Imogene wondered if she were thinking about the pearls.

She cleared her throat

Her mother turned. "Oh. Good-morning, pet! Did you sleep well?"

Imogene nodded.

"Did you want something, pet?" Mother asked. She walked over and cupped Imogene's chin in her hand, smiling. "You look a bit glum."

Imogene held out the invitation for her mother to read.

"Oh, dear!" Mother gave humorless laugh after scanning the note.

"Do I have to go?" Imogene remembered Miss Mullin's word for turning down invitations. "Can I send my regrets?"

Her mother tousled her hair and smiled again. "You don't sound very regretful." She sighed then.

"Things haven't been good between your father and your uncle lately. Frankly, I don't think your uncle is very happy. And he has always doted on you. A visit from you might cheer him up a bit. It might smooth matters between him and your father, too."

"Oh," Imogene said. The surprise of being confided in made her forget to be disappointed for a moment. It pleased her to think of herself being a messenger of good will. It put the trip in a different light. She wasn't visiting Sarah Jane, she was visiting Uncle Hugh and doing something important. She stood a little taller. "I suppose it won't be too bad."

"We should post your reply today," Mother said. "Miss Mullin can help you write a nice acceptance note. She'll take you. I'll have her buy a return ticket for Monday."

Imogene's pleasure vanished. With Miss Mullin helping her write it, the note was going to be miserable. The train ride would be torture.

"Why can't you take me?" she asked.

"I have to be here in case Mr. Holmes has news while your father is at the bank."

Voices in the hall announced the arrival of Mr. Holmes and Dr. Watson.

And Father, as well.

"Good of you to come, gentlemen," he was saying as they came into the room. "All the servants have been notified you'll want to interview them."

Imogene chewed her lower lip in vexation. She had hoped to be at the door and perhaps have a word with Mr. Holmes and Dr. Watson. Now, thanks to Sarah Jane, it was too late for that.

"Imogene," Father said in surprise. "Isn't it time for your lessons?"

"Miss Mullin has another headache." Imogene gave Mr. Holmes a meaningful look. In her list of suspects, she had underlined the part about Miss Mullin's headaches.

"Good heavens that woman has a lot of headaches," her father muttered. "Well, I'm sure you have some schoolwork to do until she revives."

"You can probably start working on your reply to Sarah Jane," Mother said with a cheery smile. To Father, she said, "Imogene has been invited to Staines for the weekend."

Father inclined his head and said, "Really."

Mr. Holmes raised a brow ever so slightly.

"Run along, pet," said Mother. We don't want to keep these gentlemen from their work."

"Pray have a seat, gentlemen." Father said.

Imogene gave a polite curtsy. Grown-ups could be so annoying.

"It's always a pleasure to meet your charming daughter," Dr. Watson said, as he sat at one end of the sofa and Mr. Holmes sat at the other. Mr. Holmes winked at her.

Maybe not all grown-ups.

Chapter Eight – A Reply and a Dreadful Poem

"What a lovely script your cousin has," Miss Mullin said. "And such a nicely worded letter! You could learn from Sarah Jane."

Imogene narrowed her eyes. "Mr. Devon is arranging things," she said, trying to keep her own voice authoritative.

But Miss Mullin was already at the chalkboard, writing. "So we'll begin with your address and today's date. Then drop down to the salutation: 'My Dear Friend.'"

"She's not my friend," Imogene said.

"More's the pity. 'My Dear Cousin,' then. Your capital C's are better than your S's or J's, so we won't try 'My Dear Sarah Jane.'"

It took three tries to satisfy Miss Mullin that the letter was presentable, and then three envelopes were wasted before she approved Imogene's script for the address.

"You can take it downstairs when our lessons are over," she told Imogene, after sealing it with brown wax. "And now I have a new poem for you to memorize."

Clearing her throat, the governess began in a raspy whine, "A fair little girl sat under a tree, sewing as long as her eyes could see; then smoothed her work and folded it right, and said, 'Dear work, goodnight! goodnight!' I'll read that again for you. 'A fair little girl . . .'"

Imogene's thoughts returned to her list of suspects. It was good that Mr. Holmes was questioning everyone, she decided. Miss Mullin would think she was safe. Then he'd ask a trick question. Then she'd have to confess.

"Daydreaming!" said Miss Mullin. Her heels clicked on the wooden floor as she came to peer at the page. "Your hand isn't improving a bit."

Just then, Dottie came to the schoolroom door and announced, "Miss Mullins is wanted in the library."

"Keep copying the poem, and say it aloud as you write it," Miss Mullin directed Imogene. "When I return, I want you to recite it for me."

When they were gone, Imogene wiped her pen nib on a cloth and put the pen and book away—she was not going to copy that stupid poem again—and went down to the hallway and put her letter on the tray of mail to be posted.

Now what?

She was tempted to go into the governess's room and look around for the pearls. Since Miss Mullin was her chief suspect, this was the perfect time.

But Dottie came up the stairs from the kitchen and said, "Miss Imogene, someone's at the kitchen door to see you. Says he wants to thank you."

Chapter Nine - Imogene and Rusty Trade Confidences

Outside, Imogene found Rusty by the rose trellis, slapping his cap against his leg, deep in thought. He brightened when he saw her.

"Yer was nice to ask yer cook to give me them sausages," he said.

"Oh. Well." Imogene lifted her shoulders.

"That's it, then. Jus' thought I'd tell yer." He kicked the grass with the toe of his scruffy shoe and stuck his hands in his pockets.

"That's very nice of you," Imogene said politely. If he was Mr. Holmes's main messenger, he probably knew tons of interesting things about the detective. He probably delivered all kinds of secret messages.

Casting about for something to say, she asked, "Where do you live?"

"By the river."

"You must see lots of interesting people."

Rusty gave a snort. "Yeah, yer could call 'em that."

"Do you have brothers or sisters," she pursued, trying to get him to talk some more.

"Just me and me mum."

"Oh." Imogene fell silent.

"So, 'oo do yer think did it?" Rusty said quickly.

"Excuse me?"

"Ain't yer Mr. 'Olmes's assistant? 'Oo do yer think took the necklace?"

"How did you know a necklace was taken?" Imogene scowled and put her hands on her hips. "You read my list!"

"Keep yer 'air on." Rusty grinned. "It's good fer a messenger to know what's going on."

"Not when it's private." Imogene felt herself flush, then, remembering she'd pried the contents of Mr. Holmes's note from Rusty.

"So what kinda necklace is it?" Rusty asked.

"It's my mother's pearls."

"Pearls! Whew!" His face lit with interest.

Imogene came closer and lowered her voice. "I think my governess did it. She's been very strange ever since they disappeared."

"Hmm," Rusty said. "Pearls is worth a lotta money. If she took 'em, she's prolly dangerous."

Imogene swallowed. "Really?" she said, hearing her voice go all breathy.

"Yeah. I'd be careful around her."

"I was thinking of looking in her room," Imogene said in a firmer voice. She was pleased to see Rusty's gray eyes fill with respect.

"When yer gets the chance," he advised, "remember, thieves 'ide things where yer least expect 'em to."

"How would you know that?"

"I 'eard Mr. 'Olmes say that."

"Oh," she said, relieved.

"So, I'll be off, then."

"Thank you for the advice," she said and, "If I find something, I'll leave a note under the geranium."

He grinned and touched his fingers to his forehead in a little salute.

And then, because ladies always sent polite inquiries, Imogene added, "I do hope your mother is well."

His grin vanished. "She ain't," he said in a choked voice.

Imogene caught her breath. "What's wrong with her?"

Rusty clamped his jaw and stared at the trellis. "She's got the fever," he finally said.

"How terrible."

A look of misery ran across his face.
"I think you should talk to our cook." Imogene said.

Chapter Ten - They Tell Mrs. Parker

"Mrs. Parker, can we talk to you?" Imogene asked.

The cook, chopping veal into small pieces, put her cleaver down. "What is it?"

"Rusty's mother is very sick," Imogene said.

Mrs. Parker peered at Rusty with interest. "What are her symptoms, lad?"

"A bad fever," Rusty mumbled. "''Er 'ead aches an' 'er stomach 'urts." He thought some more. "She can't sleep. She don't eat nuffing, either. Maggie—that's our boarder—puts a bowl of soup out on the table, but she won't go near me mum. I 'as to give it to 'er."

"How long has your mother been ill?" Mrs. Parker asked Rusty.

He frowned in thought. "She felt bad for 'bout a week, but she could still do 'er sewing. Now she don't do nuffing. 'Ad to stop sewing for the factory. She's been in bed a few days, I guess."

Mrs. Parker made a *tsk*ing sound. "This could be typhoid, lad. She should go to a hospital. She could die."

Rusty shook his head violently. "She won't go. Our neighbor's baby died in the 'ospital."

Mrs. Parker's face crinkled in concern." Did the baby have the same symptoms as your mother? Headaches? Stomachaches?"

Rusty shrugged.

"Oh, please, Mrs. Parker, do go have a look at her," Imogene urged. "You can find out how sick she really is."

After a moment, the cook said, "I'll see what I can do. Give me your address, lad." When he didn't answer, she prodded, "Is it by the river? There's nasty vapors by the river."

Rusty's mouth quivered, then smoothed in a flash. "She'll be mad at me for blabbing."

Mrs. Parker put her hands on her wide hips. "Your blabbing, as you put it, could save your mother's life. If she dies, you could end up in the workhouse. And you so scrawny, you'll not last long."

"It's on Old Mill Lane," he mumbled.

"In the docklands!"

He nodded. With a shrug, he added, "I don't know the number."

"I expect you could take me there. Although," the cook said, more to herself than to him, "It's probably a good idea to have my brother-in-law come too."

Mrs. Parker took off her apron and hung it on a peg by the door. "Imogene, find Dottie and tell her I need her to get this stew started for me."

To Rusty, she said, "You come with me. We'll take a cab to my sister's house, and then we'll see what we shall see."

Chapter Eleven - A Suspicious Piano Lesson

After lunch, there was a horrid hour of piano lessons in the parlor. The governess's headache had cancelled yesterday's music lessons, which pleased Imogene. But today Miss Mullin seemed determined to make up for lost misery. The metronome atop the piano ticked away. Imogene practiced her scales again and again.

Miss Mullin sat in one of the side chairs, embroidering a pillow cover and tapping her foot. From time to time she exclaimed, "No, no, no! Begin again! Play to the tempo! Play to the tempo!"

Imogene was sure she played her scales in perfect time. At one point she stopped. "Why can't I at least learn a melody?"

Miss Mullin snipped her thread with a small pair of scissors and secured her needle in the cloth. She leaned over her wicker sewing basket and rummaged around in it, muttering, "Where is my thimble?"

Stubbornly, Imogene waited for an answer until the governess looked up.

"You must have a sense of tempo to play a melody," she said, in a tone that suggested Imogene would never have that sense. "And you cannot play music unless you build strong fingers." She waved a hand. "Carry on."

Twinkle, who was lying near the piano stool, got up, stretched, and walked over to peer into the sewing basket. Reaching in with a paw, she batted at a tangled skein of thread.

"Get away!" snapped the governess. She shooed the cat with her hand. With a frightened meow, the cat shrank back.

Imogene jumped up and ran over to the basket. "Don't yell! She's only playing." Imogene reached down to move the basket aside and pick up Twinkle. With a speed that startled Imogene, Miss Mullins snatched up the basket.

"Keep your hands off my sewing basket," she hissed. "Get back to your lesson at once!"

Ears burning, Imogene stomped back to the piano stool, hugging Twinkle close. "Don't let her frighten you," she whispered in the cat's ear, although suddenly Rusty's words hovered in the air: *Pearls is worth a lotta money. If she took 'em she's prolly dangerous.*

Imogene placed Twinkle at her feet and began her scales again, Rusty's words echoing in her head: *Thieves 'ide things where yer least expect 'em to.*

The governess gave a little shake of her head and put her hands to her temples. "That will be all for today."

Imogene picked up Twinkle and hurried out. She went upstairs to her room, closing the door behind her. Clearly there was something suspicious about Miss Mullin's sewing basket.

Chapter Twelve - A Surprising Tea

At tea time, Miss Mullin stayed in her room. Relieved, Imogene went down to the kitchen to have tea with her friends. Maybe she would have a chance to discuss Miss Mullin's behavior about the sewing basket with Mrs. Parker. But when she reached the kitchen, there was no sign of the cook.

Of course! She'd gone out to see Rusty's mother. She must not be back yet. On the stove a pot of stew simmered. Dottie went over to it and gave the ladle a stir.

Mr. Devon stood inside the doorway, arms folded, deep in thought. He looked worried.

"Do you know when Mrs. Parker will be back?" Imogene asked him.

The butler roused himself to attention. "Good afternoon, Miss Imogene. Mrs. Parker informed me that she had an important errand to run."

Imogene gazed up at his kind, wrinkly face. Here was a chance to get to know Mr. Devon better and find out why Mrs. Parker didn't like him.

"Mr. Devon," she asked, "may I have my tea with you and Dottie?"

Startled, the butler drew himself up. "It isn't done, miss."

"Mr. Stewart used to let me."

"It's true," Dottie said from the stove, when his brows shot up. "Many's the time the four of us has had our tea here in this kitchen when Miss Mullin couldn't be bothered with her only charge. It's lonely for a girl to be left alone all the time," she pointed out.

"Well, it's highly irregular."

Imogene decided that meant "yes."

"Good," she said. She put Twinkle down and sat on her usual chair. After a moment's hesitation, Mr. Devon sat, too.

Dottie brought the tea things to the table. She served the tea and milk and sandwiches and pulled up a stool for herself. "Tuck in," she said, cheerily.

For a moment or two, Imogene savored the buttered bread. Soon she became aware that without Mrs. Parker, this was a very silent tea party. Mr. Devon stared at his teacup, munching a bite, his lined face drawn up in concern. Dottie nibbled at her sandwich, sending him nervous glances.

At last Dottie ventured, "Isn't it good weather today, Mr. Devon?"

Gravely, Mr. Devon nodded and swallowed. More silence followed.

"Don't fret about Mr. Holmes, sir," Dottie said. "He's been asking all of us all sorts of things. It's just part of his job, I expect. He don't mean anything by it."

Mr. Devon shook his head sorrowfully. "If a servant were to be the culprit, it would reflect badly on me. Although I don't believe any of you would do a thing like that . . ."

"I don't either," Imogene said loyally. To cheer Mr. Devon up, she added, "I'm glad you're our butler," then took another bite of her sandwich.

"Really?" The butler put his cup down in surprise. "Why is that?" he asked, which made her pause to come up with an answer.

"My mother says you're dignified."

A faint pink came into his papery cheeks. His mouth pulled up at the corners. "That's kind of her."

"It's true," Dottie chimed in. "I've noticed that meself."

Mr. Devon flushed with open pleasure. "We come from a long line of butlers. My father impressed upon my brother and myself when we were but lads it's important to keep a dignified manner." He leaned back a little in his chair and looked off into the distance. "When I was only eighteen . . ."

By the time Mrs. Parker returned, Dottie and Imogene were completely immersed in his latest tale about his life as a butler.

"Mind you," he said, wagging his forefinger, "I had to keep a straight face at all times." Imogene and Dottie laughed.

"What's this?" Mrs. Parker said. "Having a good time are we?"

By now, Mr. Devon seemed a younger version of himself. "Ah, Mrs. Parker," he said, rising. "That's a fine-looking hat."

The cook blushed. "Why thank you, Mr. Devon," she said. "My sister gave it to me last year." She bustled into her room off the kitchen. When she emerged, she had taken off her cape and hat. Now she donned her apron and cap.

"Have tea with us," urged Imogene, wanting the little party to last. She reminded herself to ask Mrs. Parker later what she had found out about Rusty's mother.

"Yes, do, sit down," Mr. Devon said, indicating the chair where he had sat.

"I'll put on more hot water," Dottie suggested.

Mrs. Parker smiled. "Well, only for a bit. I still have currant dumplings to make for tonight's pudding."

Imogene got up and pulled a second stool from under the table for herself. "You can sit in my chair, Mr. Devon," she told him.

And so passed one of the happiest afternoons Imogene could remember since Pilkie left.

Chapter Thirteen - Imogene Comes to a Decision

Imogene sat in the drawing room with Twinkle on her lap. Her parents sat in the two wing chairs. It was family time again.

"Did you have a nice day, pet?" her mother asked.

Imogene always said yes, since ladies weren't supposed to complain. But today it was easy to say yes.

"Did you get your reply to Sarah Jane's invitation in the post?" Mother asked.

"I did," Imogene said. She decided not to mention how many pieces of stationery had been involved.

Mother said gaily, "And what else did you do today?"

Imogene sorted through her lessons, wondering what else she could share. She could hardly say that she nearly had a row with Miss Mullen during piano time. "I'm learning a new poem," she said. Her mother liked poetry.

"Oh, recite it for us!"

Her father gave an encouraging nod. "Yes, do."

Imogene set Twinkle down and stood up, smoothing her overskirt. She got through the poem as quickly as possible, stumbling over one line, and sat down again.

"Isn't it nice that Miss Mullin is having her memorize poems?" her mother said.

"Indeed," said Father. He took a puff, and the fruity aroma of pipe smoke hung in the air.

Mention of Miss Mullin turned Imogene's thoughts to the sewing basket. She hadn't been able to talk to Mrs. Parker about Miss Mullin, because of Mr. Devon and Dottie. If only she could tell Mother her suspicions! But Mr. Holmes was coming tomorrow. Imogene could tell him and he could tell her parents.

He'd probably explain to them that she was his assistant too. How proud they would be!

" . . . and Mrs. Wrottesley wants her daughter to meet you when they get back."

Imogene roused to attention, suddenly aware of what her mother was saying.

"You'll like her, Imogene; she's a sweet girl, very close to your age. Maybe a little older."

To pretend she had been listening, Imogene asked, "*When* is this?"

"Not for a month. The Wrottesleys are going on holiday to visit relatives in Cornwall. But when they return, Mrs. Wrottesley wants to have us to tea so you and Sophronia can become acquainted."

"Sophronia?" Imogene said.

Her mother nodded. "A rather charming name, don't you think?"

"It's interesting," Imogene said politely and resisted the impulse to roll her eyes.

In a cheerier tone, Mother told Father, "I shall wear the cameo again tonight when we dine with the Butterfields."

Father took his pipe from his teeth and said, "Given Holmes's reputation, he should have the pearls found by now."

"It's only been two days, dear," said Mother. "And he is being thorough."

"Yes, yes. Going after every clue and all that."

Imogene frowned to herself, wondering exactly how she should approach Mr. Holmes tomorrow about the sewing basket.

"Imogene, I can see this business has tired you out," her mother said. "You probably should go right to bed."

Imogene quickly sat up straight. "I'm not a bit tired," she protested.

The clock on the mantelpiece struck the half hour, and Mother exclaimed, "Half-six! I didn't realize it was so late. I must go and change for dinner."

Family time was over.

After a goodnight kiss from Mother and a nose-tweak from Father, Imogene lingered at the banister, Twinkle beside her, and watched them leave. Down the stairs they walked, looking like a king and queen. Dottie arranged a velvet cape around her mother's shoulders. Mr. Devon gave her father his tall top hat, and out the door her parents went. The butler and maid melted away to other duties.

Imogene stood in thought. One day she would be going out to a dinner party, all dressed up. She would wear her silver locket instead of a cameo or pearls. And perhaps a blue silk gown, since blue was her favorite color. But her thoughts trickled sideways to an idea that had been growing throughout the day.

Except for a chance to have beautiful clothes and go to parties and the theater, like Mother, Imogene didn't want to become a proper lady. From the look of disappointment that never left Miss Mullin's face, properness made for a dreary life. Even Mother was bored at times, Imogene could tell. More than once, while having tea at an important friend's house, she had caught her mother patting a yawn.

"With all those tea parties, proper ladies don't have time to be detectives," Imogene whispered to Twinkle, who was rubbing against her ankle. "I'm going to be a detective." She put a finger to her lips and picked Twinkle up. "But that's our secret for now."

Back in her room, Imogene went through her nightly routine. She folded her undergarments and put them away in the upright chest, the way Pilkie had taught her—stockings and drawers, petticoats, camisole—and slipped her nightgown over her head. She hung her dress and overskirt on a peg in the wardrobe above the old hatbox Mother had given her to keep shawls in.

The shawls were in a jumble. The door hung ajar, too. Imogene had somehow lost the key a while back. It felt good to be careless about something that Miss Mullin would scold her for if she knew about it. The governess seldom came into Imogene's room.

She took her brush from the top of the vanity. Pilkie had taught her to brush her hair one hundred strokes each night. First, Imogene always took off her locket, so the brush wouldn't catch in the chain. After brushing, she would open the locket, kiss both her parents' photographs, and make up a little conversation for them.

Tonight, she pretended they beamed at each other and said, "Isn't Imogene a dear!" Closing the locket, she fastened its chain around her neck again, climbed into bed, and returned to her idea of being a detective. Twinkle hopped up beside her and soon was purring in a soft, rhythmic snore.

Imogene moved the cat to the other side of her pillow, careful not to wake her. Then she took the lamp from the night table and set it on the floor to hide its glow since she was supposed to be going to sleep. She picked up *Black Beauty* from the night table. Hanging over the side of the bed, with the book on the floor, she turned to Chapter Six and began to read.

It was amazing, she thought, how much she and Black Beauty felt the same. ". . . for a young horse full of strength and spirits . . . who has been used to some large field or plain, where he can fling up his head, and toss up his tail and gallop away at full speed . . . it is hard never to have a bit more liberty to do as you like . . ."

When Pilkie was here Imogene had had a kind of liberty. "Where would you like to go today, lamb?" Pilkie would say. "Which book will it be tonight?" When they read *Black Beauty* the first time, Imogene was outraged over the treatment of the horses. They talked for a long time that night about people who were cruel to animals. "You've got spirit, lamb," Pilkie said. "Always remember to stand up and be willing to set things to right."

Sleepy at last, Imogene turned off the lamp. Her last waking thought was that solving a mystery was one way to set things to right. Pilkie would approve of her being Mr. Holmes's assistant. Then she drifted into a jumbled dream where she was riding Black Beauty across a wide green meadow. Strangely, Rusty was riding Ginger at her side.

Chapter Fourteen – The Cook Shares a Plan

Imogene dawdled over her breakfast of bacon, a boiled egg, and toast, watching Mrs. Parker roll pastry for tarts at one end of the worktable. Light spilled in a rectangle across the stone floor through the open kitchen doorway. Gooseberries simmered on the stove. Mr. Devon hovered near the pot, sniffing appreciatively. Imogene wondered if she should wait until someone rang for him before asking the cook about Rusty's mother.

But that might be quite a while. "Did you figure out how to fix Rusty's mother's problem?" she finally asked.

"I did," said the cook. "I believe you said Mr. Holmes is coming today. No doubt Dr. Watson will be along. I have a plan for them to consider."

Imogene wriggled impatiently on her chair. "Tell me," she pleaded.

"Just be patient."

The front bell sounded.

"That could be the two of them now," said Mrs. Parker.

Mr. Devon adjusted his jacket, slowly made his way across the room, and went upstairs to the entrance hall.

When he was gone, Mrs. Parker said, "You know, I think Mr. Devon was just a bit shy, what with Dottie and me being here so many years ahead of him. Now that we know each other better, I can see he's not a bad sort."

"Who do you think took the pearls, then?"

"That's the mystery, isn't it." Mrs. Parker set down her rolling pin and put her floury hands on her hips. "Now, about Rusty's mother . . ."

Beyond the kitchen doorway, Imogene saw Mr. Holmes and Dr. Watson with the jobbing gardener near the stone bench under the bay tree where he had parked his wheelbarrow. Mr. Elwood held pruning shears in one hand. He shook his head; then he shrugged. Dr. Watson was writing something in a small notebook.

"I talked to my sister and her husband. You know they have a bakery, yes?" Mrs. Parker said.

Imogene nodded. Sometimes when Mrs. Parker was in a rush, she sent Jonathan to their bakery to get tea pastries from her sister.

"Well, they happen to have a small room with a special entrance. Their eldest son and his wife lived there until their own children came and they needed bigger quarters." Mrs. Parker picked up her rolling pin again. "My brother-in-law moved Rusty and his mother in last night. The kitchen door is walled up for privacy. There's no danger of germs getting into the kitchen."

Imogene opened her mouth, then closed it again, then sputtered,

"Do you mean . . . are they going to . . . she's going to stay in that room until she's well?"

"Indeed. And then my sister is thinking that room can be turned into a small sewing shop after his mum's recovered. I believe he said she sews."

Imogene nodded again, too excited to speak.

"She can begin her own shirt-making business to pay rent for living in half the attic. My sister has but the one maid-of-all-work, and it's a good-sized attic. They can live up there and his mum can have her little shop when she's well."

Unable to contain herself any longer, Imogene ran to the cook and flung her arms around her. "Oh that's grand, simply grand!"

Mrs. Parker chuckled. "So, since you're only playing with that breakfast I made for you, perhaps you can go ask Dr. Watson if he wouldn't mind coming to the door for a few minutes. Maybe I can talk him into paying a call on Rusty's mum, now she's settled in.

Imogene fairly flew out of the kitchen. She sped past the rose arbor and up the little path to the stone bench where the three men were clustered. Dr. Watson pocketed his notebook.

"I appreciate your time, Mr. Elwood," Mr. Holmes was saying.

The jobbing gardener doffed his cap. "Glad to be of any help." He pushed his wheelbarrow away from the bay tree to the box hedges behind the bench, nodding at Imogene as he passed her.

"Morning, miss."

Imogene caught her breath, and said, "Good morning." Clasping her hands together, she said, "Dr. Watson. Mrs. Parker has something very urgent to tell you, if you don't mind coming to the door."

The doctor gave a wry smile and shot a glance at Mr. Holmes. "Well, if it's urgent, I'd better go find out what it is." He walked briskly back down the path to the house. Mr. Holmes followed more slowly, Imogene at his side.

"Mr. Holmes, may I talk to you?"

"Of course," he said. "Rusty gave me your note, by the way."

"Yes, he told me."

They had reached the rosebush. Even though she thought the jobbing gardener was too far away to hear, Imogene kept her voice low, just in case. "Was Mr. Elwood able to give you any information?"

The detective considered her question, clasping his hands behind his back. "Nothing too surprising," he said at last. "Your mother had already suggested he's too old to climb up to the window. I'm persuaded he's a decent, honest chap. He assures me he would never share information about his employers."

"Why did you question him, then?"

Mr. Holmes held up a forefinger. "You must eliminate possibilities, one by one, in order to spot the right clues."

"I think I have a very important clue for you," said Imogene, flushing with pride. She told him about Miss Mullin's behavior when Twinkle had peered into the sewing basket.

"And she scolded me when I reached for the basket," Imogene finished. "She acted upset that I even thought of touching it."

The detective had listened carefully. "You don't like Miss Mullin, do you?" he said.

Imogene's mouth opened, then closed. When she found her voice, she asked, "What does that have to do with it?"

But Mr. Holmes seemed to want an answer.

"She's mean," Imogene said, and then it all came pouring out—how Miss Mullin made Imogene copy page after page, how she made Imogene play scale after scale, how she never took Imogene anywhere, like Pilkie did. How she always scolded.

Again Mr. Holmes gave her his full attention, even nodding a couple of times. "Still, a good detective is careful to consider all possibilities and not just one," he said.

"I say, Holmes," said Dr. Watson, coming out of the kitchen and up the steps. "It seems Rusty's mother is ill and the cook's sister is taking care of her. Mrs. Parker just gave me the address. She's guessing it might be typhoid, but wants my professional opinion . . ."

"Is that a toast crumb at the corner of your mouth?" Mr. Holmes asked.

Dr. Watson blushed, then cleared his throat. "Yes. Well. We'd best be on our way. Typhoid is serious business."

"And what about Mother's pearls?" Imogene asked Mr. Holmes. "If you-know-who didn't take them, who could have?"

The detective gave a mysterious smile. "There are two possibilities, and your mean governess could be one of them. But here's a question for you to think about: Is this the first time anything has disappeared?"

Imogene pondered that, then said, "As far as I know."

"Nothing else has gone missing?" he prodded. "If this is an inside job, it might not be the first time. Think about the list you gave me. Do you remember all the names on it?"

She nodded. "I made a copy of it, too."

He smiled approval. "Well done!"

Imogene felt a little thrill of pride, followed by a terrible thought. "Oh, Mr. Holmes," she said, "it can't be Dottie taking things. She would never do anything like that!"

"Holmes, we should go," urged Dr. Watson.

The detective first leaned down to whisper in Imogene's ear, "It's a puzzle you can put together, if you let your thoughts flow freely. Let ideas come to you by thinking of something else. When I'm stumped," he mused, "I play my violin."

The two men set off around the corner of the house. Imogene picked up the cat who was lying near the rose arbor and started petting her, troubled by the conversation.

A moment later, Dottie came to the kitchen door. "Miss Mullin says it's time for lessons," she announced. She turned and gave a little swish, as if she had a bustle like the governess's, and took mincing steps back inside.

Normally Imogene would have giggled at Dottie's imitation. But now she just clutched Twinkle closer and whispered, "It *mustn't* be Dottie, Twinkle. It mustn't!"

But who else could it be?

Chapter Fifteen - A Mysterious Errand and a Letter

At that moment, Elsie scuttled out the kitchen door, her eyes darting right and left. Her hand was in her skirt pocket, making a bit of a bulge. When she saw Imogene, she said, "Oh! Miss Imogene!" in little yips, as if something had bitten her.

"Elsie," Imogene said, racking her brains for a way to find out what the scullery maid was up to. "Are you all right?"

Elsie lowered her eyes, then glanced up, blinking nervously. "Please, miss. Dottie wants me to take a message for her."

"I see," Imogene said in a solemn tone, hoping she hid her amazement. "Will you be gone long?"

"No, miss," Elsie said, and when Imogene remained silent, she stammered out, "It-it's only to Jonathan."

"I see," Imogene repeated. She set Twinkle down, wondering how she might manage to ask Dottie later if this was true. "I'm sure Mrs. Parker doesn't mind."

The maid gulped. "No, miss, she don't mind a-tall. Only, maybe you wouldn't mention it . . ."

Imogene eyed Elsie's pocket and said, "Your secret is safe with me," adding for good measure, "My lips are sealed." She hadn't heard Mr. Holmes say anything like that, but according to Dottie, it was the way people talked in penny dreadfuls.

"Oh, thank you, miss! Thank you," Elsie cried.

That meant there *was* a secret. And hadn't she noticed Elsie on the first floor landing after the horrible cousins left?

"I'll be back in time to finish the pots and pans," Elsie promised.

Imogene watched the maid scurry to the far end of the wall and disappear around the corner. Then she ran to the corner herself and peered around. She saw Elsie open the side gate next to the hedge and go past the carriage house to the stable near the back. The horses' soft nickering inside the stable meant Jonathan had returned from taking Father to the bank.

Why would Elsie be taking a note from Dottie to Jonathan? Imogene's spirits plunged.

In the schoolroom, Miss Mullin seemed preoccupied. She made Imogene practice a second page of capital S's, though Imogene thought the first page looked perfectly fine. Halfway through the second page, Imogene peeked at the governess. She was reading that small torn newspaper clipping again. Her forehead crinkled as if something worried her as she put the paper back in her pocket.

During sums, Miss Mullin didn't even bother to check if Imogene's answers were correct. Instead she glanced over them quickly and muttered, "You should write more neatly. Your numbers are a disgrace," and looked off into space.

Imogene lifted her chin and said, "My father says if you can work with figures, it doesn't matter how prettily you write them." She was pleased to hear Miss Mullin gasp.

"He hasn't seen your work then," governess said, recovering. She raised her own chin. In a sweet voice that didn't match either the gleam in her eye or the sour-quince pucker of her mouth, she said, "Let's work on your poem. Your mother tells me you stumbled halfway through it last night."

Imogene fumed. Mother would never have said it in that sneery way.

"So we'll begin with, 'She did not say to the sun "goodnight!" Tho' she saw him there like a ball of light.'"

As she had the day before, Miss Mullin recited each section, making Imogene repeat it after her and write it down. Finally she handed Imogene the book, saying, "Finish memorizing it while I check the post." Miss Mullin checked the post at least three times a day, even though Dottie said no one ever wrote except the governess's married sister in Romford.

Dutifully, Imogene studied the lines, muttering them aloud: "And while on her pillow she softly lay, She knew nothing more 'till again it was day, And all things said to the beautiful sun, 'Good morning, good morning, our work is begun!'"

"Stupid girl," Imogene muttered, scrawling the words in her copybook. "Stupid sun."

Time passed, but Miss Mullin didn't return. Imogene decided to list in her diary reasons why the governess had to be guilty and Dottie innocent.

True, Elsie's visit to Jonathan was perplexing. But, thinking about it, Imogene suspected Elsie was just sneaking apples or carrots from the kitchen for the horses. She probably didn't realize Mrs. Parker wouldn't mind. Maybe Dottie's note had said something like, "Explain to Elsie the proper way to feed Cinnamon and Brownie." You had to keep your palm flat, Imogene knew; otherwise, horses might nip.

She opened her desk and pulled her diary from under the heap of books and copybooks, then let out a shocked "Oh!" The ribbon was askew, with one big floppy loop and a smaller

93

loop. This was not the bow she had tied two days ago. Miss Mullin was spying on her!

Hastily Imogene flipped through earlier pages to see what she had written. Quite a few entries were about Miss Mullin.

"For someone so skinny, when she walks, she waddles like a goose." That was at Easter.

"I don't think her French is very good. It's probably like her piano." That was just before the pearls went missing.

The thought of the governess reading her diary made Imogene clamp her teeth together so hard her jaw ached. She snapped the diary shut, wondering if Miss Mullin had seen the back page with its list of clues.

I should keep it in my room, she decided, angry with herself for not doing so earlier. Under the pillow. No, too obvious. Behind the doll's house. Yes. Who would think of looking there? Imogene stood up, marched out of the schoolroom, around the corner to the smaller hallway, and into her bedroom, muttering all the way.

The diary fit neatly between the doll's house and the wall below the window. Twinkle, whom Miss Mullin had banished from the schoolroom earlier, hopped down from Imogene's bed and ran over to investigate.

Imogene put a finger to her lips. "You mustn't tell." She picked Twinkle up, rubbed her furry chin, and sat on the bed, thinking. What would Mr. Holmes do right now? "He'd play his violin," she told Twinkle. She didn't have a violin, and she hated piano. "I wonder if you have to play scales to learn the violin."

Footsteps on the stairs made her get up and hurry out to the landing. The governess had just reached the top step and didn't seem to care that Imogene was coming from the bedroom instead of the schoolroom. Her face was flushed and almost pretty as she came around the newel post, clutching an envelope.

"You may skip lessons for the rest of the day," Miss Mullin said, catching her breath. "But do practice the rest of the poem for your mother," she added. Then she went into her room and closed the door.

Imogene tiptoed close and put her ear to the door. Inside, there was a shuffling, scraping sound as if something heavy were being pushed around. A trunk? Then a rattling sound, like drawers opening and closing. What was going on? "Why is Miss Mullin opening and closing drawers?" she whispered. "Is she packing? If so, why?"

That envelope Miss Mullin had in her hand—something must have come in the post. And Dottie would know where it was from. Imogene went down to the kitchen see what she could learn.

She found her with Mrs. Parker, huddled over the table. Dottie was giggling. The air was fragrant with the aroma of roasting lamb and bay leaf. They looked up in surprise as she entered.

"Miss Mullin dismissed class," Imogene said.

"No doubt Miss Mullin is reading her very important letter from her sister in Romford," said Dottie.

"Now, Dottie," Mrs. Parker said. She rose and went to the stove to stir the ladle inside a bubbling pot.

Dottie straightened the little white cap on her head and patted an empty chair. "Come join us, Miss Imogene."

Imogene sat and waited for Dottie to say more about the letter. When Dottie passed her a plate of tarts, she took one and nibbled it in silence.

"Awfully quiet today, miss," Dottie said. "It's not like you."

Imogene took another bite of tart, chewing it slowly, the way a calm and brilliant detective might chew while puzzling over the case. What questions would Mr. Holmes ask if he were here?

Did Dottie really give Elsie a message for Jonathan? Or had Elsie made that up? If so, what was *her* secret? Again,

Imogene thought of Sunday and Elsie's excuse for being on the first floor landing at the wrong time of day. And, If Elsie *wasn't* feeding the horses, why was Jonathan involved? But the real mystery right now was Miss Mullin's strange behavior.

"I wonder why Miss Mullin dismissed class," she finally said. "She didn't have a headache."

"It must be that letter," Dottie said. "It were a bit thicker than usual. Had a lump in it."

Mrs. Parker clanked her ladle against the pot.

"You'd best have some milk before Miss Mullin comes to get you for your piano lesson," Dottie told Imogene.

"Miss Mullin said I'm done with all of my lessons today."

"Did she now?" Mrs. Parker turned from the stove.

"She was all excited about something. I've never seen her excited," Imogene marveled.

Suddenly they heard hurried footsteps in the hallway above, steps that turned into a determined march to the front door.

"Dottie, go and see what's happening," said Mrs. Parker. Dottie flew out of the kitchen and upstairs.

"That was Miss Importance herself," she reported back to them a few moments later, breathing hard. "I ran to the front door and looked out, and there she was, heading down the street. Then she hailed a cab and got in alone!" Hands on her hips, Dottie snorted. "Din't even wait for Jonathan to escort her. And her such a proper lady!"

Chapter Sixteen - Imogene Talks with Rusty

Lunch came and went. Miss Mullin still hadn't returned.
Imogene paced in the garden, wondering how to let Mr.
Holmes know about the governess's latest behavior. "He isn't
going to send Rusty to check under the geranium pot any time
soon," she told Twinkle.

"Meow?"

"Yer allus talk to yer cat like that?"

Imogene spun around, her face hot, seeing Rusty's
broad grin.

"On our street, cats catches rats," he said.

Imogene shuddered. "Ugh!"

"But it ain't my street anymore. I come to tell you.
They moved us last night. Good thing, too. When we got back
yesterday, Maggie was gone. Left me mum just like that." He
snapped his fingers.

"How beastly of her!"

"It's a nice room yer cook's sister give me mum. And she's made me up a place in the attic." Rusty thrust his hands in his pockets. "So, thanks for poking her nose into things and telling Mrs. Parker—"

"That's a fine way to say thank you!"

"Wait. Don't get mad." Rusty held a palm out. "Maybe I din't say it right. But it's what I come to say, so I'll be off now."

"Don't leave yet," Imogene said quickly, even though he hadn't moved to go.

Imogene thought of something. "Since you're Mr. Holmes's messenger, you know where he lives, don't you. If I write a message, can you take it to him?"

"I did before, din't I?"

"Is it far from here? Is it much trouble to take it?"

Rusty shrugged. "I just 'ops on back of a carriage. They never sees me."

"Wait here," Imogene told him. "I'll be right back."

She dashed into the kitchen and up the two flights of stairs to her room. Pulling her diary from behind the doll's house, she untied the ribbon and opened the book to a fresh page. Her pen was in the schoolroom, but she found a pencil inside the drawer of the night table. Quickly she wrote, "Miss Mullin is acting strange."

Imogene stopped and chewed the end of her pencil wondering how to explain what she meant by strange. Miss Mullin looked happy for once. What did that mean? She had taken a cab alone. Did Imogene know where she went?

Imogene sighed. She closed her diary, retied the ribbon, tucked the book behind the doll's house again, and hurried back downstairs.

She found Rusty in the garden, holding Twinkle, a goofy look on his face. "She's purring," he told Imogene. Seeing Imogene was empty handed, he asked, "Where's yer message?"

"There's no point in sending it. Mr. Holmes thinks I'm wrong about my governess." Imogene put her fingers to her lips and looked across the flagstones at the kitchen door. "They don't know I'm his assistant. Let's go over to the bench."

She led him to the stone slab, and they sat down.

Rusty leaned closer. "Why don't 'e think it's 'er?"

"Mr. Holmes says I suspect her because I don't like her. He says I'm not considering all the possibilities. But she's acting more peculiar than ever." Imogene told Rusty about the strange noises from Miss Mullin's room. "And then she ran out the front door and took a cab to who knows where," Imogene finished.

Rusty's eyes were alight. "She din't say where she was going?"

"Not a word to anyone." Imogene folded her arms.

"Well, I think yer right. She prolly took the pearls."

Imogene turned to him. "Really?"

He nodded. "Jus' wait and see. 'E'll end up saying you was right all along."

Pleased, Imogene leaned closer. "I'm going to start my own detective business, after I solve this case," she said.

"All by yerself?" Rusty looked doubtful. "Safety in numbers if yer ask me. Detective work is dangerous. Ain't you noticed that Dr. Watson allus goes around wiv Mr. 'Olmes?"

"It can't be very dangerous, or Mr. Holmes wouldn't always look so calm," Imogene said. "I think Dr. Watson goes on cases with him because they're friends. It must be lonely work sometimes."

"It's dangerous work," Rusty insisted.

Later, Imogene was to remember his words.

Chapter Seventeen - New Surprises

When Imogene returned to the kitchen, Mrs. Parker was shelling peas from a bowl in her lap. For pea soup, Imogene hoped. Her stomach gave a pleased rumble. She loved pea soup.

Mr. Devon held a cup of tea in one hand and a tart in the other. Contentment lit his face as he took a bite. "Ah, Mrs. Parker," he said after swallowing. "You've a gift with pastries."

The cook beamed. "Nothing like my sister, though."

"Did Miss Mullin come back?" Imogene asked.

"Not half an hour ago," Mrs. Parker said. "She's in the library with your mother. Dottie took them tea."

Mr. Devon set his teacup down. "Shouldn't Dottie be back by now?"

"Do you want me to go get her?" Imogene asked. Without waiting for a reply, she sped from the kitchen, up the steps, and down the hallway to the library.

Dottie was listening at the carved oak door. She put finger to her lips. Imogene tiptoed closer and pressed her own ear against the door.

Mother's voice was just a soft murmur, but it seemed to fall at the end of what she had just said. Then she exclaimed, "This evening?"

Miss Mullin's high-pitched voice rose and fell excitedly. Imogene thought she heard "sister" and "Sydney."

"Who's Sydney?" she whispered to Dottie.

Dottie shrugged. "Never heard her mention a gentleman by that name. Never heard her mention *any* gentleman. She's full of surprises, that one."

They both pressed closer. Silence.

"Well, if you must," her mother said, firmer now, a finish to the matter. "I'll ring for Devon."

Imogene and Dottie both stepped away from the door into the entrance hall just as Mr. Devon came up the stairs. As he made his way to the library, they peered around the corner again. Imogene's mother and the governess had both come out of the library and were standing in the hall.

"Devon," Mother said in a cold voice, "Kindly fetch Jonathan to take down Miss Mullin's trunk and drive her to Paddington Station. She has a train to catch."

Imogene's hand went to her open mouth.

Miss Mullin swept up the hallway followed by Mother, whose forehead crinkled in dismay.

Approaching Imogene and Dottie, the governess paused and fixed Imogene with a glittery stare. "Be a good girl and remember everything I've taught you," she said. Leaning close, she hissed in Imogene's ear, "And I do *not* waddle like a goose!"

She straightened, proceeded to the entrance, her bustle wagging back and forth, and went out the front door with Mr. Devon. Imogene turned to her mother, who sighed.

"When your father comes home, I'll tell you all about it. Right now I'd like to lie down. I have a slight headache."

Dottie snapped to attention. "May I get you water, ma'am? More tea?"

"Shall I read to you?" Imogene asked, remembering that Pilkie used to read to her whenever she didn't feel well.

"Thank you, but I'll be fine," Mother said. "I just need to rest and think."

Imogene watched her mother slowly walk up the stairs.

"I don't know what to make of it," Dottie said after a moment. She fidgeted with her apron. "Your mother never gets headaches."

Imogene nibbled her lower lip, torn between hope that Miss Mullin was gone for good and anger with the governess for giving her mother a headache. What could Miss Mullin have said?

They returned to the kitchen, Dottie insisting a good cup of tea was what her mother needed.

Mrs. Parker had finished shelling her peas and was sautéing onions in a large griddle.

"Well?" the cook asked, looking from Imogene to Dottie, then back to her stove.

"Miss Mullin is leaving," Imogene said. Even as she said it, it sounded too good to be true.

Mrs. Parker moved the griddle off the flame and leaned back, hands on hips and a broad smile on her face. "Leaving, is she! And where is her ladyship going, if I may ask? A home that offers pastries more to her taste?"

"There's a gentleman named Sydney what's involved," Dottie said.

"Really!" Mrs. Parker's smile grew even broader. "Well, well, well! This evening we must be sure and give a little toast to Sydney, and wish him good fortune for taking her off our hands."

Imogene giggled. It was amazing how much freer everything already felt. No one to scold her. No disapproving sniffs. Maybe no more piano scales. She felt her mouth stretch in a smile as a new thought occurred to her.

Without Miss Mullin to take her, she wouldn't have to go to Staines Saturday.

Chapter Eighteen – Mother Shares the News

Imogene settled herself on her chair in the drawing room and waited. She recognized the expressions on her parents' faces. They had just finished talking over Something Serious.

"I have news for you, pet," Mother said at last. "As you know, Miss Mullin has left us. She's gone to her sister's home in Romford for a few days, before . . ." she trailed off.

"Where is she going?" Imogene asked. Since her mother was clearly upset about this, Imogene tried to look properly disappointed, but a balloon of happiness swelled inside her chest.

"You see . . ," Mother began again, and looked to Father.

"It seems Miss Mullin answered an advertisement in the newspaper some weeks ago." Father tamped a wad of tobacco in the bowl of his pipe. "They need wives in Sydney, and our good Miss Mullin has answered the call."

"Really, dear," Mother protested. "You needn't say it that way. It's been properly handled through the minister who's going to perform the wedding."

"Sydney?" Imogene asked.

"A city in Australia," Mother murmured. "Far away. The ends of the earth"

"Australia!" Imogene's head gave a little jolt. Her parents stared.

"Are you all right, pet?" asked Mother.

"I'm fine," Imogene said. Miss Mullin was going to the ends of the earth. It was simply too grand! She pressed her hands together and tried to compose herself.

Father turned to Mother. "From what you say, the correspondence was through her sister. How can anyone be sure this minister isn't an impostor?"

"Miss Mullin said her sister's husband had them both investigated. The groom is a sheep farmer, quite wealthy, it seems. He goes to the minister's church."

Father lifted his brows, still busy with his pipe.

"She could have given more notice." A sad look rippled over Mother's face. "I thought we were friends. I would have helped her shop for her trousseau."

Father lit the pipe and inhaled deeply, letting a cloud of fragrance into the air. "I'm sure her sister has taken care of it."

Imogene squirmed on her chair, impatient. If only they wouldn't speak as if she weren't present! Especially when they were supposed to be sharing news with her.

"Marrying someone she hasn't even met," Mother said. "I still can't believe it."

"She was tired of being *Miss* Mullin," Imogene blurted.

Father chuckled, then quickly turned it into a polite cough. Imogene saw the corners of his mouth twitch when he said, "I daresay you're right."

"That makes sense, I suppose." Mother lifted her shoulders as if it didn't explain anything.

It made perfect sense to Imogene. This was a new opportunity for Miss Mullin. She didn't like being a governess. She didn't like the servants. They didn't like her. For a moment Imogene almost felt sorry for her.

"It's a risk she's taking," said Father.

"We'll need to find a new governess," mused Mother. "What's wrong, Imogene?" she cried, as Imogene opened her mouth and snapped it shut again, then swallowed.

"Nothing," Imogene said. But a new possibility had occurred to her. Miss Mullin would soon be on a boat to Australia. She'd get a brand new name. Why, oh, why hadn't she sent that message to Mr. Holmes! Well, tomorrow she'd leave a note under the geranium pot for Rusty.

Meanwhile, there was Saturday's trip to think of, just two days away. "Do I still have to go to Staines?" she asked.

"Oh, dear," Mother said. "Hmm." She nibbled her lower lip. After a moment, she said, "I think you should."

Imogene's shoulders slumped.

"It's good to keep communication between our houses."

Father clamped his teeth on his pipe and scowled.

"I suppose Dottie could take you. Maybe Elsie can take over her work for two days," Mother mused. "I wonder if she could manage . . ."

She was interrupted by the clock.

"Gone six," said Mother. "I wish we weren't going out this evening. These dinners always have such rich food. It would be nice to stay home for a change."

To Imogene she said, "Tomorrow we'll all have dinner together, would you like that?"

Imogene brightened. "I'd like that ever so much!"

"And tonight I'll ask Dottie to eat with you so that you don't have to eat alone, now that Miss Mullin is gone."

Imogene didn't tell her that she ate in the kitchen most evenings.

Later, after dinner, Imogene paced back and forth in her room. Twinkle ran along beside her, as if it were some sort of game.

Somehow she had to get word to Mr. Holmes about Miss Mullin's sudden departure. A note under the geranium might take too long.

"I should have said something during family time," Imogene muttered. "What if Miss Mullin only *said* she would spend time with her sister? What if she's already on her way to Australia?"

Imogene took her diary from behind the doll house and tore out a page.

Dear Mother and Father, she wrote. *I have something very important to tell you. It's about Miss Mullin. I think she has the pearls. She has acted suspiciously all week, and now she's going to Australia.*

Imogene chewed the end of her pencil, wondering how to finish her note. At last she wrote, *Your Loving Daughter.* The nice thing about pencil, she thought, as she put the diary away, was that you didn't have to worry about ink splotches.

She padded across the landing and down the hallway to her parents' rooms. After a moment of indecision, she decided to leave it in her mother's room. Carefully she placed it on the pillow where her mother would have to see it. Then she returned to her room.

Finally her parents would know the truth! Feeling relieved, Imogene picked up the cat, turned off the light, and fell into a deep, dreamless sleep.

Chapter Nineteen – A New Wrinkle

The next morning Imogene was surprised by a soft hand on her shoulder. She opened her eyes groggily. Her mother was sitting on the bed beside her. Father stood in the doorway. Both were still in their dressing gowns, and both looked worried.

"We found your note, pet," Mother said. "Why are you writing us notes? What did you mean when you said Miss Mullin has been acting suspicious?"

Imogene sat up, rubbing her eyes. Then she told them about the sewing basket and how Miss Mullin's headaches were probably a good excuse for her to go into Mother's room.

"She's the only one that had the upstairs to herself, when everyone was downstairs," Imogene said. Well, except for Aunt Letitia being late at breakfast, but that was just Aunt Letitia. "And Miss Mullin got a new headache just about every time Mr. Holmes came. I think she had a guilty conscience."

"Oh, dear," Mother said. She looked at Father. "It does sound suspicious."

114

Father nodded. "I'll have Jonathan take a message to Mr. Holmes."

"No," said Mother. "Have Jonathan fetch him. We need to tell him what has happened and see what he plans."

When at last Mr. Holmes was ushered in and greetings were made, the detective sat down on the sofa and crossed his long legs.

"Where's Dr. Watson?" Imogene asked.

"Visiting a patient," he replied.

To Father he said, "Your man said it was urgent. It's good he came when he did. I was just getting ready to leave for the train station." His expression unreadable, he added, "There are a few points I still need to check."

"I hope Miss Mullin is one of them," said Mother. "She left us last night. She's gone to visit her sister before leaving for Australia."

"Australia?" He tapped his fingertips together and looked into space. "Hmm. This is a new wrinkle. Why Australia?"

"She's going to marry a rich sheep farmer," said Imogene.

Mother set her chin. "That's what she told us. She may just be running away with my pearls."

"This does support one possibility," Mr. Holmes mused.

"As far as I'm concerned, there's *only* one possibility," Father said. "Miss Mullin has gone off suddenly, and we haven't found the pearls."

"Do you know which boat your governess is taking? Or where it leaves from and when?"

"She only said she would spend some time with her sister in Romford before sailing," Mother said. "When I think how I trusted her!" she added bitterly.

"Romford. That's not *too* far from the Docks. But a good way from here."

"I wanted to send you a message," Imogene said, the words spilling out of her. "I heard Miss Mullin moving her things around in her room. And Dottie saw her get a thick letter. And then Miss Mullin went out and hailed a cab with no chaperone—" Imogene stopped, aware all three were staring at her. Only Mr. Holmes wore an amused smile.

"Imogene has been assisting me in this case," he said. "She's come up with some fine clues for me."

Imogene flushed with pleasure.

"Imogene?" asked Father.

"Assisting you!" Mother said.

Mr. Holmes leaned forward, resting his hands on his knees. "This changes my plans somewhat. I'll check the docks for ship schedules and passenger lists. Perhaps you can visit the sister in Romford, Mrs. Walters, and talk to your fleeing governess if she's still there."

"I don't want my wife or my daughter near a dangerous criminal," Father said.

"From my earlier interview, I would say your Miss Mullin is of a hysterical nature and not at all dangerous," Mr. Holmes said. "If she took the pearls, it was a desperate measure. If your wife shows up with Imogene, Miss Mullin is likely to confess on the spot."

"I'm definitely going," Mother told Father. "I plan to give that woman a piece of my mind. We can have Jonathan drop us at Paddington after he drops you at the bank."

Imogene jumped to her feet, tumbling Twinkle to the floor. "I'm coming, too," she insisted. When Father shook his head, she said, "It's only right. I'm Mr. Holmes's assistant. I can notice things Mother might miss."

A new smile flitted across Mr. Holmes's face.

"I want Jonathan with you, then," Father said firmly. "I'll take a cab to the bank, and Jonathan can come for me this afternoon.

Mr. Holmes rose. "If everything is settled, I'll be on my way."

"I'll walk with you to the door," Father said.

When the two men had left the room, Mother turned to Imogene.

"I'll have to tell Mrs. Parker we may not be back for lunch." She put a finger to her lower lip. "Oh, dear. I know Miss Mullin's sister lives in Romford, but I don't actually know the address."

"Dottie will know," Imogene said.

Chapter Twenty - Off to Catch a Thief

Dottie did know, and soon Imogene and her mother were sitting across from each other in the carriage, heading for Romford, with Jonathan urging the two bay horses as fast as they could go. The horses' hooves drummed against the metaled roadway. The carriage shook. Scenery went by in a blur. Imogene folded her hands tightly. Despite their speed, she worried they might not make it in time. What if the governess had sailed last night?

Mother's hands were balled in angry fists. Imogene had never seen her like this. She was looking out the window in that unseeing way grown-ups sometimes had when their thoughts were elsewhere. Once or twice her lips moved, as if she were saying something to someone that Imogene couldn't hear.

A picnic basket sat on the floor between them. Mrs. Parker had insisted on packing tarts and sandwiches from yesterday's lamb roast.

Imogene couldn't imagine being hungry on such an exciting trip. They were going to nab a thief. She had known all along it was Miss Mullin. She was glad that Mr. Holmes finally realized it too.

As the carriage finally pulled up before a three-story brick house, Imogene wondered if Dottie had been mistaken about the address. Whenever Miss Mullin had mentioned her sister, she made it sound as if she lived on a huge estate. Imogene had expected a long road to an immense mansion in the distance.

Her mother checked the scrap of paper where she had written the address.

"This is it," she said, sounding as surprised as Imogene felt.

Jonathan alit and came around to the carriage door.

"I don't think we'll be long, Jonathan," Mother said, as he helped her and Imogene down.

He straightened the driving jacket he'd donned for the journey. "I'll be right here, madam," he said.

Imogene followed her mother up the short walk and the five steps to the portico, where her mother rang the bell. A moment later the door was opened by a barrel-chested, whiskery butler who looked them up and down and growled, "Yes?"

"We're here to see Mrs. Reginald Pemberton."

"Is she expecting you?"

Imogene's mother smiled prettily and said, "No, but we came to give her sister our best wishes for a good journey. I'm Mrs. Harland Walters, and Miss Mullin was our governess. She packed in rather a hurry when she left yesterday. I'm afraid we didn't say proper goodbyes."

The butler ushered them inside and into the morning room, saying, "Wait here please," then vanished down a long hall.

A few moments he reappeared and said," Please come this way." He led them into a drawing room off the far end of the hallway, where a stout woman with a round face and flouncy curls came to meet them. The skirt of her dress was layered in pink ruffles, and each layer was trimmed in ivory lace.

How could this woman possibly be scrawny Miss Mullin's sister? Imogene wondered.

Mrs. Pemberton made that clear by frowning her disapproval and asking in a familiar, scraping voice, "To what do I owe this visit, Mrs. Walters?" She swept a chilly gaze over both Imogene and her mother.

"Do sit down," she added in a voice that suggested she'd be much happier if they turned around and left. She indicated a chintz sofa and armchair. They both took the sofa.

"Shall I ring for tea?" Mrs. Pemberton asked in that same discouraging tone.

Imogene's mother shook her head. "We won't be long. We just wanted to wish Miss Mullin *bon voyage*. Would you mind sending for her?"

Mrs. Pemberton gave a little wave of her hand. "You've missed her. She left not two hours ago for Tilbury Dock. She's taking a rather long voyage."

Imogene's mother gasped. Then, in a wondering tone she asked, "You didn't see your sister off?"

Mrs. Pemberton stiffened. "My footman drove her to the dock and will see her safely embarked."

"But she's going to Australia," Mother said. "To be married."

"To a sheep farmer," Imogene chimed in.

Mrs. Pemberton's eyes narrowed. "A wealthy sheep farmer, Mrs. Walters," she said, confining her gaze to Imogene's mother as if Imogene were invisible. "I would never have bought the tickets nor given her travel money if I thought there was anything to worry about. My husband and I had the bridegroom investigated. A thrifty man with no bad habits.

He's only looking for a good English wife. It's all gone through the minister who is going to marry them. We had him investigated as well."

"Australia is so far away." Imogene's mother said.

Mrs. Pemberton shook her head. "My sister wasn't happy being a governess, Mrs. Walters." She looked at Imogene. "She never enjoyed it. Frankly, I was tiring of her complaints."

Imogene was tempted to say, *So was I*, but bit her tongue.

"I don't know what there was to complain about," Mother said coldly. "I treated her very well, and Imogene is well-behaved."

"My sister never expected to have to work, Mrs. Walters. When I married, I had a handsome dowry, but when our father died, everything went to our brother, and . . ." Mrs. Pemberton shrugged. "When she showed up with that advertisement from the paper, well! She was so insistent." Mrs. Pemberton fidgeted with one of her ruffles. "Are you sure you won't have some tea?" she asked.

"You're very kind, but we can't stay," Imogene's mother said. "But perhaps you could tell us which ship she is taking?"

"Yes. *The Petrel*. On the Orient and Pacific Line." Mrs. Pemberton glanced at a clunky dark clock on the mantelpiece with scenes of cherubs painted all around the clock face. "You might still be able to catch her. The boat leaves from Tilbury Dock at noon."

"We won't take any more of your time, then," Imogene's mother said. "And how kind of you to help your sister in her endeavors."

Mrs. Pemberton gave a stiff smile. "What are sisters for?" She rose and walked to the bell pull by the fireplace. A moment later the butler showed them to the door.

Hurrying to the carriage, Mother told Imogene, "We *do* have time if we hasten!

"Jonathan," she directed. "You've got to get us to Tilbury Dock. Go as fast as you can."

As Jonathan helped her and Imogene into the carriage, she muttered to Imogene, "What are sisters for indeed! They probably planned it together!"

Chapter Twenty-one - Chasing Miss Mullin

Jonathan took Mother's words to heart. The carriage rattled and bumped along streets and roads as the horses galloped faster and faster to their destination. Mother stared moodily out the window.

Imogene clasped her hands together, her thoughts veering between worry over the horses—it was just such a run that had made Black Beauty's loose shoe come off, damaging his hoof—and a surprising wave of sympathy for Miss Mullin.

Didn't anyone like the governess? Not even her own sister? Mrs. Pemberton sounded glad to be rid of her. Imogene had longed for a sister or brother. But between the horrid cousins and Miss Mullin's sister, now Imogene was glad she was an only child. Still, Mrs. Pemberton had paid for Miss Mullin's ticket. That was something.

The carriage turned onto a long street that ran between shops and market stalls down to the river at the far end. The air was rackety with people calling wares, shoppers bargaining, the clip-clop of horse hooves, the rattling wheels of traps and horse-drawn omnibuses. Imogene craned her neck out the window, looking this way and that.

Mother leaned forward. "We're almost there," she said, a catch in her voice. "I hope they haven't raised the gangplank."

"What's a gangplank?" Imogene asked.

"A walkway that leads from the quay to the ship's deck so the passengers can board the ship."

Ahead, through the window, Imogene saw three rough-looking men laughing loudly outside the doorway of a shabby corner building. Then a man with a kerchief tied around his head came sauntering along the cobblestones. How odd he looked!

At that moment, a carriage trundled out of a side lane and cut in front of them so fast it teetered from side to side, blocking their way. The two black horses pulling it reared up, whinnying shrilly, and the carriage turned over, sending a stack of barrels flying from a nearby doorway. Imogene felt their own carriage rock, the bays dancing sideways, neighing frantically, as Jonathan brought them under control and the carriage lurched to a standstill.

A row broke out between the owner of the barrels and the other coachman, as the man inside the overturned carriage climbed out, straightening his frock coat. Shopkeepers and customers alike surged around them, eager to see what would happen next.

Their angry voices were drowned out by a sudden loud blast of a horn from the river.

"The ship is leaving!" Mother said, and opened the door. Jonathan leaped down to help her, then Imogene from the carriage.

"Maybe we can still catch Miss Mullin," Imogene said.

She grabbed Mother's arm, and they both set off at a run, Mother holding her hat with one hand. They came out onto the dock.

"They've cast off!" Mother said. Her mouth turned down in dismay.

Imogene looked from her mother to the three long quays stretching out into the gray water of the port. Two were empty, but a crowd had gathered at the middle one. Some people waved at a huge ship that was moving away. The ship had three tall masts and what looked like a smokestack. Passengers on the ship's deck waved back.

"Quick!" Imogene said, and she tugged her mother's arm, hurrying to the quay and pushing through the well-wishers to the front. To her surprise, a familiar tall, thin figure stood watching the boat, his hands clasped behind his back.

"Mr. Holmes!" she said.

"Mr. Holmes," Mother echoed.

He turned.

"Is there any way we can have the ship called back?" Mother asked.

He shook his head. "It's too late for that." The three watched quietly as the gray waters between the ship and the quay grew ever wider.

"We were so close to catching her," Imogene said.

She scanned the ship deck, trying to see if the governess was there. It was hard to tell. She squinted her eyes—and there was Miss Mullin, a tiny figure in a brown traveling suit with a matching hat, her posture a prim line of correctness even now as she stood at the rail.

After a moment, Mr. Holmes said, "I believe our business here is concluded. And now I must get on with other matters."

"But my pearls!" Mother said.

Mr. Holmes said calmly, "If evidence points to Miss Mullin having them, we can wire ahead and have her detained for inquiries on arrival. It's a forty-six-day trip. We have time."

"Mother," Imogene said slowly, on their way back to the carriage, "The more I think about it . . . ." It was hard for her to admit the thought that had worked its way into her mind.

"Yes?"

"Miss Mullin's sister paid for her ticket and she's going to marry a rich man. What I mean is, Miss Mullin doesn't really have a reason to steal."

"Imogene, you can't mean that!"

Mr. Holmes was at Imogene's side. "Quite a good observation," he said.

Her mother gave him a cold look. "I'm not sure one needs any motive except greed to become a thief."

"True, but Miss Mullin is a bit old to start stealing if she hasn't had a history of stealing before now. Whereas . . ." The detective didn't finish, but merely pursed his lips.

A tear trickled down her mother's cheek. Her mother quickly brushed it away. "They were my wedding pearls," she told Imogene softly.

"You may yet get them back," Mr. Holmes said.

"Hallo. Here we are," he added, as Jonathan drew up in the carriage and stopped.

The detective helped them both into the carriage. "I expect to have the case solved shortly, Mrs. Walters," he said. "And Imogene, I think you should trust your observations and perhaps check your list again."

He closed the door, tipped his hat, then set off walking in the direction of the railway station.

It was a silent ride home. Imogene and her mother ate Mrs. Parker's sandwiches, each lost in her own thoughts.

Why did Mr. Holmes mention the list? Mentally Imogene went through it again—butlers never did it. Mrs. Parker wouldn't. Dottie wouldn't. Elsie was only trying to clean because Aunt Letitia wouldn't let her earlier, if she was to be believed. Now it looked like Miss Mullin had no reason to steal. The jobbing gardener was too old to climb the downpipe, and Jonathan wasn't on the list.

So it was someone inside. Or someone who had been inside.

The bite of sandwich Imogene had just taken suddenly tasted like wadded paper. A queasy feeling in her stomach made her put her sandwich down.

She knew who had the pearls.

Chapter Twenty-Two - Rusty Makes an Offer

As soon as they arrived home, Imogene ran upstairs and pulled out her diary to see exactly what she had written. She sat on the bed next to Twinkle and turned quickly to the back. When she scanned the page, the words fairly leaped out at her: *Aunt Letitia was late to breakfast. But she always goes down late. That's nothing unusual.*

Only this time Father had refused Uncle Hugh a new loan.

"It's a good thing I'm going to Staines, Twinkle," she said, then bit her lip. What exactly would she do when she got there? She had to find the pearls. But how?

Imogene put the diary back, then scooped up Twinkle. The garden bench was a good place to sit and think.

Mrs. Parker was in the kitchen, cutting up lamb for cutlets.

"Rusty was looking for you a while ago," she said. "He might be in the garden, or he might have gone home. Poor lad. My sister says his mother is still in a bad way."

"Thank you." Imogene nodded distractedly and went on out the back door.

At the foot of the steps, she spied Dottie and Elsie at the rose trellis, their heads close together. Neither of them saw her.

"Do you have them?" Dottie asked.

Elsie shook her head. "This morning he sez he coon't go to the bank till later, 'cuz it's all topsy-turvy today what with the trip to Romford."

He. That had to be Jonathan. What was Elsie supposed to have?

Suddenly both maids became aware of Imogene staring at them.

"Miss Imogene!" Dottie said.

"Miss Imogene!" Elsie echoed. "She knows," she told Dottie.

"Oh, miss," Dottie said in a coaxing voice, "Don't go telling on me to Mrs. Parker. You know she don't approve of my reading them. Jonathan gets them for me after he takes yer father to the bank. I gives Elsie the money and she gives it to him . . ."

Books! Elsie was taking money for Jonathan to buy penny dreadfuls!

Imogene let out a slow breath. "I won't say a word," she promised.

"How was yer trip?" Dottie asked. "Did you find the pearls? That's all anyone can talk about today."

Imogene shook her head slowly. Seeing their disappointed faces, she said, "It's a long story."

"Come on, then," Dottie said to Elsie. "We'd best get back to the kitchen before Mrs. Parker comes looking for us."

Imogene found Rusty waiting for her at the bench. He was walking back and forth, slapping his cap against his leg from time to time, his brow furrowed in thought. His ginger hair was still ragged, but it was a bit shorter. Mrs. Parker's sister must have gotten out her scissors.

"Did you catch yer governess?" Rusty asked, as soon as she drew near. "I 'eard yer maid talking about 'er leaving fer Australia."

Imogene sat down and started petting Twinkle glumly. "She's not the thief."

"She ain't!" Rusty sat beside her. "'Oo is, then?"

Imogene hesitated. In a burst of confidence, she told him, "My aunt in Staines."

"Whew!"

"I don't know how to tell my parents," Imogene said, looking down. "Mother still thinks it's Miss Mullin. They won't believe it could be Aunt Letitia."

"Mr. 'Olmes will."

"I think he suspects her, too," Imogene said slowly. "But he can't search her house, so how can he find them? I'm sure she's hidden the pearls there somewhere."

She looked at Rusty. "I'm supposed to go to Staines tomorrow for a visit, so I'm going to look for them. Once I get them, we'll have proof."

Rusty's forehead scrunched up. "That's kinda tricky, ain't it?"

Imogene lifted her shoulders. "Dottie will be with me. There's nothing to worry about."

He studied her for a moment. "When's yer train."

"Sometime after eleven. We're supposed to be there about noon."

"Paddington station?"

"Waterloo, I think." To change the subject, Imogene said, "Mrs. Parker says you were looking for me."

"Yeah." Rusty cleared his throat and slapped his cap against his leg again. "Uh, yer know the detective business yer wants to start? I think yer needs a partner."

"Why would I need a partner?" Imogene asked in surprise.

"It's dangerous to work alone."

"I wish you'd stop saying that."

"Jus' think," Rusty plunged on, his face flushed with excitement. "I can go all over the city to find out stuff and report back to yer. What's yer last name again?"

"Walters. Why?"

"We can be the Russell and Walters Detective Business."

"Russell?"

"That's my last name."

"Walters and Russell," Imogene said immediately.

"It should be alphabetic."

"Alphabetical," she corrected him.

"Russell and Walters *is* alphabetical." At her cross look, he said, "We can think of a name we bof likes. Anyway, I gots ta get going."

"I haven't said I want a partner," she called after him as he started up the path to the trellis.

He looked back at her and gave her a lopsided grin before he went on his way.

Chapter Twenty-three - Imogene Tells Dottie Her Plan

"We could each have one now," Imogene coaxed. "Just one won't spoil our lunch."

She and Dottie were on the train to Staines. Across from her, Dottie asked, "Don't all this rocking make you queasy, Miss Imogene? I coon't think of eating a cherry tart, but you go ahead." She fished out a packet from her large bag, the upside-down-flowerpot-shaped hat on her head jiggling a little. She unwrapped the package and handed a tart to Imogene along with a small napkin.

Imogene looked around the interior of their first class coach while she munched the flaky pastry, savoring its juicy filling.

Waterloo station had been crowded and noisy. The train had been late. Now that they were aboard, their private coach reminded her of the family carriage, except that the leather and trim were brown and cream instead of black, and the wheels went clickety-clack instead of rattling. A gas lamp was fixed over each seat, unlit. Sunlight poured through the window.

They had left the outskirts of London. Imogene could see scattered fields and trees under a blue sky with milky clouds. In the distance, red and gray house roofs gleamed. Once she saw a church spire.

"I don't mind the rocking," she told Dottie. Feeling a sugary smear on her lower lip, she dabbed it with her napkin. "It's not nearly as bad as yesterday," she added. "Yesterday we galloped everywhere."

Dottie tucked the bundled tarts inside her bag again and made a soft tsk-tsk.

"All that trouble for nothing. And now our ladyship is on her way to Australia anyway with yer mum's pearls."

"Miss Mullin doesn't have the pearls," Imogene said. She had debated with herself all morning about how much to tell Dottie. "I know who does."

Dottie's dark eyes rounded. She straightened in her seat. "Who, then?"

"Aunt Letitia." Imogene lowered her voice, even though there was no one else to hear. "And I'm going to steal them back."

"Oh, miss!" Dottie put a gloved hand to her mouth, then took it away and leaned forward. "Please don't try that, miss.

Yer auntie's a cold one. Cold and hard, if you'll forgive my saying so, being as how she's a relative. I don't think you want to cross her."

"She's not a relative," Imogene said with some heat. "Not a real one, anyway."

Dottie was silent.

"If I'm careful, she won't know until it's too late," Imogene assured her. "We'll be back in Kensington before she finds out."

"You don't know that. It's just like in *The Stolen Necklace.*" Dottie colored slightly and fidgeted with a button on her summer coat. "Jonathan got it for me yesterday. The title got his attention, with yer mum's pearls being on everyone's mind and all."

Imogene asked, "What happens in *The Stolen Necklace?* Did someone's aunt steal a necklace?"

"There's no aunt in the story a-tall, miss. Lord and Lady Crawchester visit an old friend at his mansion in the country. It's a very old house, with a trap door that Lady Crawchester don't know about until someone starts tapping from below . . ."

"I don't think there's a trapdoor in my uncle's house," Imogene said, feeling a creepy tickle on the back of her neck.

She hoped that was true. Uncle Hugh had moved from

his smaller house in town when he married Aunt Letitia. Imogene and her parents had been to the new house twice. It was on the edge of town, behind a stone wall and down a long carriageway from the main road. The house was awfully big, Imogene reflected. It could be full of hidden surprises. Whenever they visited, she noticed the servants were a little jumpy.

All except for Aunt Letitia's lady's maid, Dora. The tall, bony, dish-faced woman had piercing black eyes, and the two times Imogene had seen the maid, she never once smiled. The other servants seemed wary when she was in the room.

"I don't know how you can find them pearls, even if yer auntie do have them," Dottie said, her gaze still anxious.

Imogene took a slow breath so that she would seem calm and confident when she spoke. "I have a plan, Dottie. I need your help."

"Me?" The maid gave a nervous laugh. "How can I help, Miss Imogene? Likely I'll be downstairs most of the time with the servants."

"I'll tell them you're our lady's maid, now, and that Mother spared you for the weekend, and you have to come up to my room to comb my hair and help me dress."

Dottie pursed her lips. "I hope Elsie don't make a hash of things while we're gone. Her mind is such a muddle sometimes." She cocked her head, coming back to what Imogene had just said. "So I'm to brush yer hair, am I?"

"It's a good excuse for you to come to my room."

Dottie grinned. "It does sound a bit exciting, in't it? We'll be like Mr. Holmes, looking for clues an' such." Her grin faded. "You'd do better to tell Mr. Holmes what you think and let him take care of it."

For a moment Imogene was tempted to tell Dottie she was Mr. Holmes's assistant. But that would sound like bragging. Instead she said, "I'm planning to have a toothache at tea. Then, while everyone's downstairs, I can look in Aunt Letitia's room until I find the pearls."

Dottie's breath caught. "What if she catches you in her room?"

"What can she do to me?"

"She can tell yer parents you snoop in other people's rooms."

"She won't catch me," Imogene insisted. "I'll be quick. I know I'll find them."

"And where do plan to hide them after you take them? She'll be sure one of us did it." The maid knitted her brows in thought. "Pockets is the first place she'd check."

"True," Imogene said, remembering Rusty's explanation of why he put everything under his cap. She took an absentminded bite of her tart, not really tasting it as she chewed and thought.

"I can put them inside my camisole and tie a ribbon tight around my waist under my dress," she said. "When I find the pearls, I can drop them down the neck of my bodice. She'd never think to check there."

Dottie's face brightened momentarily. "That's clever, Miss Imogene. It could work. The ribbon will keep them from slipping down, and the ruffles on yer bodice can hide any bulge."

"And then I'll keep having my toothache so bad that we have to change our plans and come home tonight."

That taken care of, Imogene settled back on her seat to comfortably finish her tart.

Dottie quietly took a small yellow-backed book from her bag. Imogene just had time to see the picture on the front was of a woman whose eyes were wide with fear, when Dottie opened the book and began to read. A moment later she snapped the book shut.

"Miss Imogene, don't do it. Anything might happen. Tell Mr. Holmes and let him handle it."

Imogene set her chin. "I'm counting on you, Dottie." She folded her napkin and put it into the pocket of her traveling jacket.

"But . . ." the maid began.

The train was slowing down. Through the window, a brick building set back from a wide platform came into view. Among the few people waiting on the platform, Imogene spied Sarah Jane and her governess, Miss Wicks.

"We're here," Imogene said. "And Dottie . . ."

"Yes, miss?"

"If you discover anything . . , you know, if the servants there tell you anything I should know, raise one eyebrow at me."

Her forehead still puckered in worry, Dottie nodded and re-fastened her dark hat with her hatpin.

"Really, Dottie, nothing will go wrong," Imogene assured the maid. She tied the sash of her own small, flowered hat under her chin. A shiver of excitement ran through her. This must be how Mr. Holmes felt when he was about to finish a case.

Chapter Twenty-four - Imogene Explores and Waits

"Where's your governess?" Sarah Jane asked Imogene. She looked Dottie up and down, as the coachman lifted Imogene's small trunk. Fingering the lace trim on her cape, she said, "How disappointing for Miss Wicks. She was so hoping for a visit with Miss Mullin. Weren't you Miss Wicks?"

Miss Wicks, a pretty young woman with ginger curls peeping out from a rather plain bonnet, bobbed her head. Her darting eyes and dimples seemed to suggest she hid a lively disposition behind her meek smile.

"Miss Mullin is on a ship to Australia," Imogene said.

"Australia!" Sarah Jane looked pop-eyed.

Dottie carried her own carpetbag as they all went down the platform steps to the waiting brougham, where the coachman helped each of them inside. Shortly after he started off, Imogene's felt a thump against the back of her seat.

"What was that?" asked Dottie, startled.

"I didn't hear anything," Sarah Jane said, looking bored. She and the governess sat across from them. "Why is your governess going to Australia?" she asked Imogene.

On the rest of the trip, Imogene gave a brief version of Miss Mullin's departure.

Sarah Jane sniffed. "A sheep farmer!"

"And he's very wealthy." Imogene said.

A shadow ran over her cousin's face.

The brougham slowed a little to go through the open wrought-iron gates, then rattled down a tree-lined driveway between hedged gardens, stopping in front of the looming stone house. A waiting footman opened the door and handed them down. They followed him up the stairs into a marble foyer where Mr. Noseworthy, the thin, overly deferential butler, stood at attention after letting them in.

Imogene received a warm hug from Uncle Hugh, then a stiff one from Aunt Letitia. Dora, forbidding as ever, stood near an ornate table, glancing at calling cards on a silver tray.

Imogene explained all over again why Dottie had come instead of Miss Mullin.

"It's actually better Dottie's here," Aunt Letitia said. "In the yellow room," she called after the footman, who was taking Imogene's trunk upstairs.

To Dottie she said, "One of our maids was called home for an emergency. You can help serve lunch."

"Dottie's our lady's maid now," Imogene said.

"Lady's maid!" Sarah Jane turned in surprise. "Has she had proper training?"

In a bright and cheerful voice, Dottie said, "I'll be glad to lend a hand, madam. Miss Imogene can ring whenever she needs me."

"Dora will show you to the servant's hall, then."

"May I wash up and change?" Imogene asked, thinking it would be good excuse to take a quick look around the upstairs rooms.

"Sarah Jane, why don't you take Imogene to her room?"

As they went up two flights of carpeted stairs, for the sake of conversation, Imogene asked, "Where's Perry?"

Sarah Jane's lip curled. "Having a picnic in the back field with Nurse. Then he'll run around and catch butterflies for his stupid collection. He sticks pins in them, you know."

Imogene could think of no reply to that.

They turned into a hallway on the left. "Here's your room," Sarah Jane said. She ushered Imogene into a large room wallpapered in a pattern of swirly green leaves with pale yellow flowers. Imogene's trunk sat at the foot of the canopied bed.

"Maybe Dora can show Dottie how to fix your hair like mine," Sarah Jane said, patting the twist of ringlets on her head. "You can borrow one of my combs." It seemed a generous suggestion until she added, "I can't think why your mother doesn't find a proper lady's maid who knows how to do hair."

"I like my hair the way it is."

Sarah Jane flashed a sudden, mean smile. "Yes, I forgot. You're not old enough to wear it this way. Would you prefer to eat outside with Perry and Nurse?"

Mr. Holmes's words in the garden came back to Imogene: *A good detective doesn't let emotion cloud reason.* I'm here to find Mother's pearls, she reminded herself. She would ignore anything Sarah Jane said.

"I'm looking forward to lunch with you," she told Sarah Jane. According to Miss Mullin, ladies sometimes told social lies. For once her advice seemed useful.

Sarah Jane lifted her brows. "I'll meet you downstairs then. You'll find the water closet on the other side of the stairwell and fresh hand towels. Don't take too long."

"Thank you."

A fine hostess! Imogene thought, after her cousin flounced out the door. She wondered why Sarah Jane had even invited her, though she was glad to be left alone at the moment. She took out the lavender-flowered skirt and bodice she'd packed on top in her trunk and hurriedly changed, carefully tying one of her ribbons tightly around her camisole. Then she slipped out of the room and wandered into the carpeted hallway.

She tiptoed to the room across from hers. Turning the doorknob carefully, she peeked in and saw a gentleman's dressing chest, just like Father's. Her aunt's room must be the one closer to the end of the hall. Imogene silently closed her uncle's door and started down the hall.

To her surprise, the door at the very end opened and Dora emerged from the servant's stairs. Imogene's heart did a little somersault.

Dora's eyes narrowed. In a raspy voice that seemed full of warning, she asked, "Is there something I can help you with, Miss Imogene?"

"I . . , I was looking for the water closet," Imogene stammered.

"This way, miss." Dora passed her, indicating with a nod that Imogene should follow her up the hall and to the corner room across the landing.

"Here it is," she told Imogene. "And the bath is next door."

"Thank you," Imogene said.

"So now you know where everything is," Dora said, and her eyes seemed to drill into Imogene's head.

"Yes."

"You'll want to hurry, miss. They're waiting lunch on you."

Imogene went into the room and slid the dainty brass bolt. Then she ran water at the sink bowl and washed her hands and freshened her face, drying them with a soft towel on the rack by the door. When she came out again, Dora was gone.

The afternoon seemed to drag on forever. Over a luncheon of brisket of beef and suet dumplings, conversation had been stilted. Afterwards, Uncle Hugh said he had work to do at his office. Nurse came in briefly to say she was taking Perry to the river to feed bread to the ducks. Aunt Letitia retired to her room, saying she had letters to write, which meant Imogene couldn't go upstairs again for fear of running into her.

Instead, she sat, hands folded, in the drawing room on the sofa, while Sarah Jane played piano. Beside her, Miss Wicks quietly read a book in French. Occasionally she looked over and smiled at Imogene. Once she held a finger to her lips, suggesting that one couldn't speak while Sarah Jane played. Then she rolled her eyes.

Imogene stifled a smile, then frowned to herself. How unfair that a mean girl like Sarah Jane had such a nice governess, while she had been stuck with a grouch like Miss Mullin.

Her thoughts were interrupted by Dottie coming into the drawing room to water the fern on the plant stand by the window. As she passed Imogene on the way out, she raised one eyebrow. Imogene sat up a little straighter. Dottie had found out something.

Maybe she could tell Miss Wicks her jaw ached and she wanted to lie down. That would give her a good reason to go upstairs and ring for Dottie. It might even make her toothache more convincing later. Imogene was just about to lean over and whisper to the governess, when Sarah Jane abruptly stopped playing.

"I feel like a game of draughts," she told the governess.

"I was planning to go outside to finish my watercolor in the back garden," Miss Wicks said. "Perhaps your cousin would enjoy a game."

"Do you play draughts?" Sarah Jane asked Imogene as she took the board and pieces from a drawer in the highboy and set them on a small table between two chairs.

Imogene was tempted to say no, but everyone knew how to play draughts, even Perry. "Yes," she grumped, and she could hear her own irritation.

Miss Wicks quickly left the room with the air of someone escaping. Over the next hour, Imogene found out why. Sarah Jane was a poor loser, haggling with Imogene whenever she jumped one of her pieces. It was a relief when Uncle Hugh returned from his office.

With an indulgent, "Hello, girls," he settled into his easy chair and immersed himself in the newspaper. For a while Sarah Jane played in sullen silence and Imogene was free to think of the coming search for her mother's pearls.

Aunt Letitia finally swept into the room, wearing a peach and beige silk dress gathered in swirls. The dress rustled as she walked over to the fireplace and yanked the bell pull.

Uncle Hugh eyed her outfit, a pensive look on his face, as she sat in an armless chair, carefully lifting her bustle.

"Tea," she said, with a wave of the hand when Dottie appeared. "Where's Miss Wicks?" she inquired of Sarah Jane who was putting the draughts game away.

"Doing one of her watercolors. Let her keep painting. She can be tiresome at tea."

When Dottie rolled in the tea cart a few minutes later, Imogene jumped to her feet. She clapped a hand to her jaw and moaned.

"Is something wrong?" Uncle Hugh asked. He leaned forward, brows puckered.

"My tooth hurts," Imogene said, and she scrunched up her face. "Right here," she said, pressing her hand just below her cheek.

"Why don't you go lie down, miss?" Dottie quickly suggested. "I'll get you some laudanum tea as soon as I return to the kitchen."

Imogene nodded, her hand still pressed against both cheek and jaw. She curtsied to her aunt and uncle and went slowly out the door, shoulders hunched, as if that helped the pain.

Once she reached the staircase and knew she was out of their sight, she dropped her hand and straightened her shoulders. Then she ran up the two flights of stairs, eager to get started on her search.

Chapter Twenty-five - The Pearls!

In her room again, Imogene felt her waist to make sure her ribbon was in place. She sat on the bed, waiting for Dottie. A few minutes later the maid came in, holding a cup of steaming tea on a saucer.

Dottie set the tea on the night table, whispering, "I had to make them think you really need it so I could come upstairs. But please, miss, don't go through with this. There's more than yer mum's pearls involved. Cooks and maids talks when they goes grocery shopping, an'—"

"What did you find out?" Imogene interrupted, trying to keep her voice low despite her excitement.

"Word has it jewelry disappears from homes here in Staines, right after yer auntie pays social calls."

Imogene widened her eyes.

"An' that's not all. The cook has a cousin what knows the butcher's daughter in Falmarsh where madam lived with her first husband. There's talk that jewelry disappeared there, too."

Imogene blinked. "That's a lot of stealing."

"So you see, miss, it's best to finish out yer visit and not do any of what you said on the train. When we goes home, you can tell Mr. Holmes what you think and let him handle things."

"But I'm right here," Imogene argued in a whisper. "And I can get into her room."

The maid fidgeted with her apron, her eyes troubled. "Then whatever you do, don't drink the tea. Laudanum makes you sleepy, and you'll need to keep yer wits."

"I won't take even a sip," Imogene promised.

"I'd best get back," Dottie muttered nervously. "It's not good to be gone too long."

After Dottie left, Imogene stole down the carpeted hall, her heart fluttering as she opened the door to Aunt Letitia's room. She closed it behind her and glanced around.

Bed, writing table, and trunk at her left. In front of her, a long wardrobe. What a lot of clothes Aunt Letitia must have! A long key stuck out of the keyhole in the middle panel. At each end of the wardrobe was a small drawer close to the floor.

Against the wall to Imogene's right a marble-topped vanity table was littered with brushes, combs, bottles, and an enameled box. Imogene hurried to the box and opened it. To her disappointment, it held only hatpins. One by one, she opened the side drawers. Gloves, stockings, corset covers. Creams, powders, combs, ribbons.

Next she looked through the drawers in the dresser: Petticoats, bustles, corsets, camisoles, evening purses. The top drawer held jewelry boxes. None of them had the pearls.

Where could they be? Imogene looked again at the wardrobe and the low drawers at each end. It would be odd to keep jewelry in either one, but those were the only drawers she hadn't tried.

The first held only scarves. The second was locked. Imogene took the key from the center panel and tried it in the lock, chewing her lower lip in worry. But it turned with a click and she smiled to herself. The drawer scraped a little as she drew it out.

What she saw made her gasp. A pair of glowing red earrings lay next to a bracelet of sparkling yellow stones. There was a cameo brooch. A jet bead necklace. Jet earrings. A string of blue beads. Jumbles of other jewelry under that. A small bundle was tucked against one corner of the drawer—

something wrapped in a silk handkerchief. Imogene lifted it gently, feeling several round bumps through the silk.

Slowly she unwrapped the handkerchief and caught her breath. There they were—her mother's pearls, pale and gleaming in the soft white cloth.

The cloth fluttered down to the drawer as Imogene pinched the neck of her bodice, pulled it out a little, and dropped the pearls down her front. She felt them snuggling against her waist where she'd tied the ribbon so tightly. She adjusted her ruffles, pleased that nothing showed, then hurriedly started to push the drawer in, but the cloth snagged.

Detectives stay calm, she told herself, but her heart speeded up. She rocked the drawer back and forth a little until the cloth loosened and she could push the drawer all the way in. Relieved, Imogene locked the drawer, stood up, and put the key back in the main panel keyhole.

She had just smoothed her overskirt and was starting for the hall door, when it was opened by Aunt Letitia. For a long moment they stared at each other.

"I came up to see how you were feeling." Aunt Letitia's mouth drew to one side in a knowing smile. "But you weren't in your room."

When Imogene didn't answer, the smile vanished. "Why are you snooping in *my* room?"

Aunt Letitia came closer, grabbing Imogene's arm, then looked slowly around the room—first at the wardrobe door, then the lower wardrobe drawers, then the vanity drawers, then the dresser, where her gaze rested on a middle drawer that hadn't gone in all the way. "You've been going through my things!"

Holding Imogene's arm in a grip that Imogene was sure would leave bruises, Aunt Letitia pulled her to the wardrobe, took the skeleton key in her other hand, and inserted it the drawer where Imogene had found the pearls. She yanked out the drawer with a strength that alarmed Imogene.

"I see," she said, when the empty silk handkerchief came into view. "What did you do with them?" Her grasp tightened.

Determined not to cry, Imogene said, "Do with what?"

"Don't play games with me, you silly child." Aunt Letitia shook her. "You've taken my pearls."

"They're not your pearls," Imogene said vehemently. Immediately she knew her mistake.

"So you did take them," Aunt Letitia said. "Empty your pockets!"

From some inner instinct, Imogene allowed herself to dart a glance at the writing table with its flat middle drawer.

Then she looked down and carefully pulled out her pocket linings.

"I see," Aunt Letitia said again. "So, you've hidden them." Her gaze wandered to the writing table. "Thought you'd come back for them, did you? Planning another toothache?"

Imogene was silent.

"I'll find them," Aunt Letitia said.

A gentle cough at the door made them both turn. The butler hovered at the threshold, his face expressionless.

Aunt Letitia frowned. "What is it, Noseworthy?"

As if he didn't notice her tight grip on Imogene's arm, he inclined his head and said, "Madam, there's a Mr. Sherlock Holmes here to see you."

"Mr. Holmes!" Imogene's heart lifted.

"Have Mr. Walters deal with him," Aunt Letitia said impatiently.

"I believe he especially wants to speak with you, madam."

Imogene thought Aunt Letitia paled a little.

"Tell Mr. Holmes—" Imogene began, but her aunt's sharp voice cut her off.

"Tell Mr. Holmes I'll be right down, Noseworthy."

The butler inclined his head again. "Yes madam," he said, and was gone before Imogene could send any message.

Aunt Letitia turned to her and said in a very different voice, "Tell me where you hid them, and I'll say nothing about it. Your uncle doesn't know about them. And I don't think your parents would like to hear you've been in my room, trying to steal my emeralds," she warned. "You'd be wise to cooperate with me."

Imogene clenched her fists and glared. "I'm going to tell them everything. You stole those other jewels, too, didn't you!"

Aunt Letitia's eyes narrowed. In a casual gesture, she reached over and opened the wardrobe door. Grabbing Imogene by the hair, she shoved her inside. In the enveloping darkness, Imogene heard the key turn before her aunt removed it. A faint light filtered through the empty keyhole. On the other side, Aunt Letitia said, "I don't believe you'll tell anybody anything."

Imogene flung herself against the door, but it didn't give. Banging on it, she yelled, "Let me out! Let me out this minute!" She took a deep breath and screamed as loudly as she could.

When she stopped to take a second breath, Aunt Letitia said, 'No one can hear you, dear. They're in the drawing room. Nurse and Perry are feeding ducks. Miss Wicks is in the back garden."

Imogene's mouth felt suddenly dry.

She could almost hear the sneer in Aunt Letitia's voice when she said, "Well, I mustn't keep Mr. Holmes waiting."

Then there was silence.

The hot, stuffy air inside the wardrobe pressed in on Imogene. A scent of lilac mingled with the mustiness of worn clothes and perspiration. Imogene's thoughts raced in every direction. Whatever Aunt Letitia was planning, she had to find a way to defend herself. She felt around in the gloom. Only clothes and hat boxes.

Hatboxes! Maybe one of the hats still had its hatpin.

Chapter Twenty-six - A Visit from Dora

A moment later, Dora's raspy voice floating through the keyhole. "I just saw yer auntie, miss. You shouldn't have ruffled her feathers like that."

If only to squeeze away her fright, Imogene said angrily, "She's not my aunt." Her hands shaking, she lifted a box lid and ran her fingers over a hat's fake flowers. No hat pin. She eased the box down and felt for another.

"I been yer auntie's lady's maid ever since she were fifteen . . ."

Another flare of anger made Imogene brave. "She's a mean, wicked person."

"She's always been good to me."

In the dim light, Imogene ran her fingers over the feathers of a fake bird on a hat. Near one of its wings she felt a tiny glass knob. A wave of relief washed over her as she pulled the hatpin out. She put her eye to the keyhole, then jumped back. Dora's glinty eye peered back.

"Why don't you just tell us what you did with yer auntie's pearls?" asked Dora.

"Those are my mother's pearls," Imogene said, recovering. She jutted her chin. "And Aunt Letitia is a thief. I saw those other jewels."

After a long moment, Dora said in a voice that was almost a growl, "We can't have you going around saying things like that, can we?"

"It's stupid to steal things and then stick them in a drawer, anyway," Imogene said.

Dora gave a raspy laugh. "They aren't in the drawer long. I have a cousin in Bristol helps us sell them." Her voice dropped even lower. "What are we going to do with you, I wonder?"

A fluttery panic nearly took Imogene's breath away. Why hadn't she listened to Dottie and let Mr. Holmes handle this? Why hadn't she listened to Rusty? Then she remembered Mr. Holmes was downstairs.

"You'd better be careful," she warned. "Mr. Holmes is here, and I'm his assistant."

"And I'm the Queen of England." This was followed by another raspy laugh.

Imogene kicked the door in frustration.

"Dora said. "Maybe you'll have a sip of laudanum after all. And maybe you'll fall down the stairs. Hmm. All kinds of possibilities. I'll think of something," Dora promised.

"You don't scare me," Imogene said, even though Dora did.

"I'll be back. Don't go away, now." A thin ray of light through the keyhole suggested the maid had gone away from the door.

In the dim light, Imogene clasped the hatpin, trying not to shiver. *Were* Aunt Letitia and Dora just trying to frighten her? Or would they really do something? What good was a hatpin?

A moment later, a familiar voice whispered through the keyhole, "See? I told yer yer needs a partner."

Chapter Twenty-seven - What Hatpins Can Do

"Rusty!" Imogene said, and then clapped her hand over her mouth, not knowing exactly where Dora had gone.

"Shhh," he hissed. "Do you know where I can find something sharp?"

She made herself become businesslike. Detectives were calm. "Would a hatpin work?"

"Yeah."

"There's a few in that box on the dresser."

After a moment of rustlings, mutterings, and tinkles of discarded pins, Rusty was back at the keyhole, whispering, "This should do."

Imogene peered through hole and saw two hatpins waving and pressing and stabbing.

"How ever did you get here?" she asked.

"Got off the train when yer did and 'opped on the back of yer carriage."

Imogene remembered the thump she and Dottie had heard as the coachman set off from the station. A warmth like sunshine flowed through her, mixed with relief. "That was you!"

She was answered by a low grunt.

"Where have you been all this time?"

"Waiting for Mr. 'Olmes and the doctor. Last night after you told me what yer was going to do, I told Mr. 'Olmes. and 'e said 'e had business 'ere today anyway."

"Oh. But . . ."

"I gots-ta concentrate," Rusty muttered.

"Sorry." Imogene pinched her lips together to keep from talking. Relief at Rusty's arrival started to give way to anxiety about Dora's return.

At last there was a click-clack of the lock turning, and the wardrobe door swung open. Imogene had never been so glad to see Rusty's good-natured, freckled face.

"Yer a mess, ain'tcha," he said cheerily, as he helped her out of the wardrobe. Seeing the hatpin she held, he added in a low voice, "Yer got pluck, I gives yer that! C'mon, let's go."

They stole out of Aunt Letitia's room, both clutching their hatpins, and looked up and down the hall. Rusty jerked his head toward the stairs.

"Where did you wait all this time?" Imogene whispered, as they made their way up the hall.

"Went to the back and asked the cook could I work for sumfing to eat. She sent me to 'elp the groom sweep the stable. When I 'eard them talking about a cab out in front, I figgered it were Mr. 'Olmes, so I come looking fer you."

"Didn't anyone see you?" Imogene asked, as they started down the stairs.

He shrugged, looking pleased with himself. "I'm good at not being seen."

A sudden exclamation made them stop and turn. At the end of the hall, Dora had just come through the servants' door, holding a small bottle. Her face red with outrage, she came running toward them, surprisingly fast, despite her long skirt.

For the second time that afternoon, Imogene opened her mouth and screamed.

"C'mon," she said, grabbing Rusty's hand, and then the two of them went pell mell down the stairs as fast as they could.

When they reached the first floor landing, Imogene paused a moment to look back and immediately regretted it. Dora was just a few steps behind them.

"Don't stop!" Rusty yanked her hand and they were running again.

They were just two steps short of the ground landing when Imogene felt fingers knot in her hair and yank her backward.

In a flash, Rusty turned and jabbed at Dora's other hand with his hatpin.

"I'll get you, you little . . ." Dora dropped her bottle and tried to hang on to Imogene, but Imogene pulled free. She stumbled down the last two steps and let out another loud scream, even as she saw the worried faces of her uncle, Mr. Holmes, Dr. Watson, and a police constable, as they hurried up the hallway. Aunt Letitia and Sarah Jane followed more slowly. Sarah Jane was crying.

Rusty turned to Imogene. He shook his head grinned. "Blimey you gots a bully scream!"

"Rusty?" Mr. Holmes said, looking more surprised than Imogene had ever seen him.

Rusty grinned and touched fingers to his forehead. He pulled his cap out of his pocket and slapped it against his leg.

Just then a bony hand clamped down on Imogene's shoulder. Dora had recovered and, despite the fact that her breath came in short gasps, her grip felt like iron. Her other hand grasped Rusty by the hair.

"Mr. Walters, sir," Dora said to Uncle Hugh. "I caught these two in madam's room, trying to steal her jewelry."

The constable gave Dora a chilly smile. "Are you sure about that?" he asked.

He walked closer, his polished black boots thudding on the patterned carpet, the buttons of his high-collared coat catching the light. In his hands were a pair of handcuffs.

"I'm more interested in the stolen jewelry your cousin in Bristol has been selling."

"I can't help what my cousin does," Dora said, managing to sound offended. "He's a ne'er-do-well, and always has been. I've avoided him for years."

"He says he gets a regular supply from you and your mistress," Mr. Holmes said. "We've talked to him more than once, and he's signed a confession."

"It's no use, Dora," said Aunt Letitia.

Only then did Imogene notice that Aunt Letitia's hands, resting against the sash of her skirt, were cuffed. Imogene broke free of the maid's grasp and went up to Mr. Holmes.

"I found them," she said. He raised his brows.

She turned away and leaned over. Reaching into her bodice, she pulled out the precious string of pearls.

"Your mother's pearls!" Uncle Hugh said. He turned to Aunt Letitia, his face registering disgust. "How could you!"

Mr. Holmes took the pearls, and an odd bark that might have been a laugh escaped him. Carefully he wrapped them in a handkerchief and put them in his pocket.

"Well done, Imogene!" he said. "Very well done indeed!" He frowned then.

"But you must promise not to do dangerous things like this in the future. This could have turned out badly for you."

"Yes, sir," Imogene said. On her next case she was sure she would be more careful.

Chapter Twenty-eight - On the Train to Waterloo

"Since nobody really had tea," Dottie said, "maybe someone would like one of Mrs. Parker's tarts."

They were on their way to Waterloo station. Imogene and Dottie had packed while Aunt Letitia and Dora were signing written confessions in the drawing room. A second constable joined the first, and they took the women to the constabulary station. At the Staines telegraph office Mr. Holmes had wired ahead to Imogene's parents for someone to meet their 8:54 arrival.

At the mention of tarts, Rusty's face lit up. Squashed between the window and Dr. Watson, he'd been examining the train's private carriage, running his finger along the wood trim and taking everything in. The gas lamp above the rocking seat cast a yellow glow on his face as he licked his lips and said, "I din't have lunch neither."

On the other side of Dr. Watson, Mr. Holmes roused himself from private thought and told Dottie, "That's kind of you, but I'm not quite ready for food."

Dr. Watson gave a polite cough. "If there's enough to go around," he said.

A moment later, Dottie had passed tarts and napkins out, declining to eat one herself. "I gets a little seasick on a train," she explained.

Imogene nibbled her tart, thinking she could hardly wait to be home and see her mother's face when they gave her the pearls.

Dottie said, "I was so worried, miss. When I heard that scream, my heart nearly stopped."

"It's good that Rusty was there," Imogene said. She shot him a grateful glance and was rewarded with a cherry-smeared grin.

Dr. Watson nudged Rusty. "You're the hero of the day, lad."

"They both were heroes," Mr. Holmes said.

"Mr. Holmes," Imogene asked, around the warm glow his words gave her, "how did you know Aunt Letitia was the culprit?"

"Ah." The detective leaned back against the upholstery, crossed his thin legs, and steepled his fingers. "I started to suspect her when your list showed she was late to breakfast."

Embarrassed, Imogene said, "I should have suspected that, too."

"She counted on her behavior seeming normal to the family. On the other hand, as you pointed out, Miss Mullin was the one behaving suspiciously, which was why she was my second suspect. But your governess had no history of stealing—I visited her previous employer. And you figured out for yourself that she had no reason to steal the pearls."

"I should at least have been suspicious about Aunt Letitia after Father told you he wouldn't loan Uncle Hugh any more mon—" Imogene clapped a hand to her mouth.

"Yes, I know you heard that when you listened at the door." Mr. Holmes gave her a wry smile. "I spent much of the week looking into their finances after that conversation, including a few visits to the constable in Falmarsh where your aunt previously lived, and the bank in London where she kept a private account. Then there was the cousin in Bristol."

"Dora told me about him," Imogene said, and she repeated the conversation.

"To think her and Dora was stealing from people all that time!" Dottie pinched her lips.

Imogene stared out at the dark, shadowy scenery flowing by. She felt a peculiar mixture of exhaustion buoyed with excitement. "At least we got the pearls."

Doctor Watson leaned forward. He brushed crumbs from his mustache with the napkin and said kindly. "I'm sure your mother will be glad to have them back."

Imogene fell silent, wondering what would happen to Sarah Jane and Perry and Aunt Letitia, now that Uncle Hugh knew Aunt Letitia was a thief. A *common* thief. Strangely, the word gave her no pleasure.

"Hallo, we're here," Mr. Holmes said. The train, with a harsh grinding of wheels slowing on the rails, entered the noisy station. A few minutes later, he and Doctor Watson handed Imogene and Dottie down and collected their bags.

While they were busy, Rusty pulled Imogene to one side.

"I 'ave a name fer our detective business." When she didn't answer, he said, "C'mon. After today I should be yer partner."

Imogene nodded. "All right. But remember, the business was my idea. What's the name, then?"

"WalRus Detective Business. See, the W and R is capitals," Rusty explained, his eyes shining. "Short for Walters and Russell. And Walters comes first, jus' like you wanted."

"That's clever," Imogene said. "Peculiar, though. It makes you think of the animal."

"That's the point," Rusty said. "We'll have a picture of a walrus wif his long teefs, see?" He held his hands apart in the air to show her. "And the words, 'We gets our teefs into cases.'"

Dr. Watson came up and put a hand on Rusty's shoulder. "I'd best take this lad to his mother. That will give me a chance to see how she's doing."

"I'll accompany the ladies and explain things to Mr. and Mrs. Walters," Mr. Holmes said.

"That's really clever," Imogene called as the doctor and Rusty walked off. Rusty turned and flashed a grin.

"Here's Jonathan," said Dottie.

"Miss Imogene," said Jonathan. He touched his hat. "Dottie."

For a moment Imogene saw his shy glance linger on Dottie's face before he led them to the waiting carriage that would take them home.

Chapter Twenty-nine - Imogene and Holmes Tell All

Imogene's parents were hovering anxiously at Mr. Devon's side when he opened the door.

"Your telegram didn't explain the reason for this unexpected arrival," Imogene's father said to Mr. Holmes.

Her mother asked, "Did something happen, Imogene?"

"Mr. and Mrs. Walters, there is much to tell," the detective told them. "Perhaps we might go into your drawing room?"

"As they followed the butler, Imogene whispered to Mr. Holmes, "I can't think how to tell them. It's so awful."

"We'll both tell them," he said in a calm, reassuring voice.

In the drawing room, Mr. Holmes declined coffee, but accepted a brandy from Father. Mother rang for tea and sat down, her face apprehensive. Mr. Holmes sat at one end of the sofa and Imogene sat on a chair by the table.

"Dottie should stay, too," she said. "She was part of everything that happened."

"Oh, dear," said Mother. "Something did happen."

When Elsie rolled in the teacart and Mother poured a cup for herself, there was a brief, polite chat about weather.

Then Mr. Holmes leaned forward and said, "About the pearls . . . I have good news for you, but I have bad news as well."

Father pulled at his mustache, his forehead drawn up with worry.

"Could we hear the good news first?" Mother asked.

Mr. Holmes took a strand of gleaming, ivory pearls from his pocket.

Mother gave a small cry. "You found them." With a radiant smile that lifted Imogene's heart, she took the pearls and fastened them around her neck. "Where on earth were they?"

"Your daughter found them," Mr. Holmes said. "But that brings us to the bad news. They were hidden in a drawer in your sister-in-law's bedroom."

A shocked silence met his words.

"Oh, my!" Mother finally said.

"My brother!" Father briefly closed his eyes. He pressed a thumb against his teeth, creating a weird grimace.

"Your brother's *wife*," Mr. Holmes corrected him. "Your brother had no part in this."

And then he and Imogene took turns telling what had happened, with Dottie at times adding a detail.

When Imogene got to the point where Aunt Letitia had locked her in the wardrobe, Mother gave another little cry and came and stood beside her. With her mother's arm around her, Imogene told how Rusty had freed her from the wardrobe and how they gotten away from Dora.

Mother dabbed her eyes. "I never would have insisted that you accept Sarah Jane's invitation if I had the slightest inkling."

"I'm glad I went. I found your pearls, And, thanks to Rusty, I was able to get away."

"Who is this Rusty?" Father asked.

"The boy who delivered my message Wednesday morning," Mr. Holmes said.

"I met him in the kitchen," said Imogene. "He's ever so nice."

A little pucker appeared between Mother's brows.

"A good lad," Mr. Holmes said. "His mother is a widow. Right now she's very ill. Your cook's sister has kindly taken them both in. Your daughter may have saved the woman's life."

Imogene's parents both turned to her.

"Rusty's going to start school soon," Imogene said.

"I'll let you handle this," Father told Mother." He poured himself another glass of brandy. "How is Hugh taking it?" he asked Mr. Holmes.

"Shaken, as you can imagine. Although, no doubt his finances will recover now," the detective added drily.

"What about my sister-in-law and her maid?"

"They're in the custody of the Staines police, after signing confessions."

Devon came to the doorway and announced, "Mrs. Parker has prepared a light supper in the dining room."

"Would you care to stay?" Mother asked Mr. Holmes.

"Yes, I find my appetite is quite recovered," he said. "I would be most obliged to accept."

They moved to the dining room, where platters of cold beef and cheese and fruit had been set out. Mr. Devon began pouring wine. A glass of milk was by Imogene's plate. Dottie had hurried down to the kitchen where, Imogene suspected, she was relating the day's events to Mrs. Parker and Elsie.

Imogene was surprised to discover how hungry she was, now that she was safe again. For a while she was too absorbed in chewing and swallowing to say much.

When they had finished dishes of Mrs. Parker's baked custard pudding and the detective was consulting his pocket watch, Imogene said, "May I ask a question, Mr. Holmes?"

"You may."

"What is the name of your detective business?"

He looked up. "I have a consulting *agency.* Why do you ask?"

While Imogene debated whether to tell him, Father took his own pocket watch from his waistcoat.

"I know it's late," he told Mr. Holmes, "I can settle your expenses now in my office, or tomorrow when I return from the bank."

"Tomorrow will be fine."

Mr. Holmes rose, as did the others, and Imogene decided to keep her plans to herself for the present.

When Father and Mr. Holmes left the room, Mother turned to Imogene.

"About Rusty . . ."

Imogene clasped her hands, waiting for the kind of lecture about street boys Miss Mullin would probably have given.

Instead, Mother said, "I see I'll have to pay more attention to what goes on in this house. Is he well behaved, this boy?"

"He's very polite. He can read, too," Imogene said hurriedly. A new idea occurred to her, thinking of how Rusty had spent the afternoon while he waited for Mr. Holmes.

"Maybe Father could hire him to be a sweeper in the stable."

"Why should he do that?"

"Jonathan has too many things to do."

"True." Mother frowned in thought. "I need to thank this boy," she said at last. "And I suppose I should call on his mother when she's well."

"She might be terribly busy," Imogene said. "She sews."

"Really?" A faint smile replaced Mother's frown. "For a living?"

"When she's well, she does." That was true enough, Imogene told herself, even if Mrs. Russell only did piecework. Remembering what Mrs. Parker had said, Imogene added, "She might start her own shop."

After a moment's silence, Mother smiled again and put a finger to her lips. "Don't tell anyone," she said, with a confiding air that thrilled Imogene, "but a visit with her might be a nice change from all these society ladies."

"Oh, may I go with you? Please?"

"Yes, of course," Mother said. In a softer tone, she said, "You know, there are times I miss my father's tailor shop."

Imogene stood very still, aware that she was on the edge of discovery.

"It would be nice to do something more useful than going to tea parties." Mother straightened and set her mouth in a firm, but not happy, line. "Oh, there are the charity bazaars. And I found an art lecture about Pissarro quite interesting. And I do like the theater, but . . ."

Imogene gulped. Since mother was being so honest, this might be her chance to say what she really felt about things.

"Mother, when you hire a new governess," she said, all in a rush, "please get me a nice one this time; a jolly one who *likes* children and really teaches me things. Miss Mullin scolded me no matter what I did. I couldn't do anything right, and—"

Mother hurried to Imogene's side, her skirts rustling. She put her arms around Imogene and drew her close. "Oh, my pet," she said, softly. "I see we must have a good long talk."

Imogene plunged ahead. "And I don't want to be called 'pet' anymore."

"Why ever not?"

At her mother's look of astonishment, Imogene said, "'Pet' is for children. For very *small* children."

"Ah." Her mother looked away, several expressions chasing themselves across her face before she nodded.

"Yes," she said, slowly. "I see. What do you want me to call you then, p—?" She stopped herself. "What shall I call you then?"

Imogene thought a moment.

"Just call me Imogene, please."

The End

Acknowledgements

Many thanks to Nathan and Mary Harrell-Bond, who took me to the Sherlock Holmes Museum in London a few years ago, lighting a spark of imagination that led to this story.

Thanks, too, to friends who read early drafts and gave good feedback: Terri and David Anderson, Craig and Melanie Briggs, Michelle Fayard, JaNay Brown-Wood, Geri Hart, Rick Asherson, and Maya Samuels-Fair.

Special thanks to my fellow members in the Storytellers writing group. They gave valuable critiques of *numerous* drafts: Rosi Hollinbeck, Nancy Herman, Susan Britton, Randall Buechner, and Jennie Hansen.

I'm also grateful for the wealth of research information I found available on the Internet and people who corresponded with me, answering my questions.

To name a few:

Dawn Whitehead and Peter Thorpe, Visitor Services Assistants, National Railway Museum - Search.Engine@ScienceMuseum.ac.uk

Gillian Simpson, Public Enquiries Librarian, Australian National Maritime Museum gsimpson@anmm.gov.au (The ship called the *Petrel*, however, is purely my invention.)

John H. Andela's blog and follow-up correspondence, *The Art of Age of Sail* - www.ageofsail.net

Lee Jackson's blog and follow-up correspondence *Victorian London* - http://www.victorianlondon.org/lee/about_the_author.htm

Tom Wareham, Enquiries, the Museum of London Docklands –http://www.museumoflondon.org.uk/docklands/

Mike Sussex at *Fonte dei Marmi, London* – http://www.fontedeimarmi.com, answered many questions about Victorian Era bathrooms and plumbing.

Robert Fleming posts articles about the Victorian Era, on his blog, *Kate Tattersall Adventures* http://www.katetattersall.com/?cat=1 and answered questions about Victorian pastimes.

Dr. George Landow, Founder, Chief Editor, and Webmaster of *The Victorian Web* – http://www.victorianweb.org, and Dr. Jacqueline Banerjee, Associate Editor, were also helpful in answering numerous questions.

Last, but not least, I found the following books so helpful:

Flanders, Judith, *Inside the Victorian Home*, New York, London: W. W. Norton & Company, 2003

Flanders, Judith, *The Victorian City*, New York: Thomas Dunne Books, St. Martin's Press, 2014

Bradshaw's Handbook, 1863 (Bradshaw's Descriptive Railway Handbook of Great Britain and Ireland), Oxford: Old House Books and Maps, 2012, http://co.uk-www.com/oldhousebooks.co.uk

The Annotated Sherlock Holmes, Vol. I and II,, edited by William S. Baring-Gould, New York: Clarkson N. Potter, Inc., Publisher, 1960

Mrs. Beeton's Book of Household Management, originally published in 1861 by O. S. Beeton Publishing; now online at http://www.mrsbeeton.com as part of an ongoing project providing free access to the complete text.

About the Author

Elizabeth Varadan is a former middle-grade elementary teacher who lives with her husband in Sacramento, California. She is an avid reader of mysteries, especially if Sherlock Holmes is involved. *Imogene and the Case of the Missing Pearls* is her first mystery novel for readers ages 8-12. Previous work has been published in *Story Friends*, *Ladybug*, and *Skipping Stones*, and she is the author of a fantasy novel, *The Fourth Wish*, also for readers ages 8-12.

You can visit Elizabeth online at

http://victorianscribbles.blogspot.com and

http://elizabethvaradansfourthwish.blogspot.com ,

or at her author page on Facebook,

https://www.facebook.com/ElizabethVaradanAuthor

Also from MX Publishing

MX Publishing is the world's largest specialist Sherlock Holmes publisher, with over a hundred titles and fifty authors creating the latest in Sherlock Holmes fiction and non-fiction.

From traditional short stories and novels to travel guides and quiz books, MX Publishing cater for all Holmes fans.

The collection includes leading titles such as *Benedict Cumberbatch In Transition* and *The Norwood Author* which won the 2011 Howlett Award (Sherlock Holmes Book of the Year).

MX Publishing also has one of the largest communities of Holmes fans on Facebook with regular contributions from dozens of authors.

www.mxpublishing.com

Also from MX Publishing

The Amazing Airship Adventure:
The Macdougall Twins with Sherlock Holmes Book #1

From the bestselling team of Derrick Belanger and Brian Belanger comes a fun filled mystery adventure for kids of all ages. It is London, 1897, and a pleasant dinner with a very special friend, Sherlock Holmes, is shattered by a terrific explosion that plunges 10 year old twin detectives, Emma and Jimmy MacDougall, into an adventure that threatens all they know and love. A mad man, possessing a remarkable airship the size of two circus elephants, threatens not only the famous 221B Baker Street house, but all of England, even the world! The great Sherlock Holmes cannot solve this mystery alone. It is up to the MacDougall twins, to use their wits and amazing detective skills, to find the hidden airship and foil the plans of the Mad Airship Bomber!

www.mxpublishing.com

Also from MX Publishing

Lego Sherlock Holmes

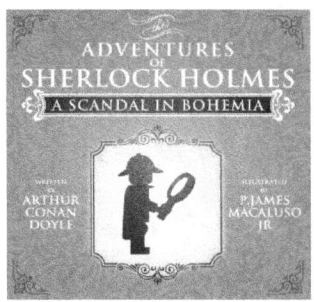 

Six original adventures from Sir Arthur Conan Doyle, re-illustrated in Lego.

In this book series, the short stories comprising The Adventures of Sherlock Holmes have been amusingly illustrated using only Lego® brand minifigures and bricks. The illustrations recreate, through custom designed Lego models, the composition of the black and white drawings by Sidney Paget that accompanied the original publication of these adventures appearing in The Strand Magazine from July 1891 to June 1892.

www.mxpublishing.com

Also from MX Publishing

Our bestselling books are our short story collections;

'Lost Stories of Sherlock Holmes' , 'The Outstanding
Mysteries of Sherlock Holmes', The Papers of Sherlock
Holmes Volume 1 and 2, 'Untold Adventures of Sherlock
Holmes' (and the sequel 'Studies in Legacy) and 'Sherlock
Holmes in Pursuit', 'The Cotswold Werewolf and Other
Stories of Sherlock Holmes' – and many more……

www.mxpublishing.com

Also from MX Publishing

"Phil Growick's, 'The Secret Journal of Dr Watson', is an adventure which takes place in the latter part of Holmes and Watson's lives. They are entrusted by HM Government (although not officially) and the King no less to undertake a rescue mission to save the Romanovs, Russia's Royal family from a grisly end at the hand of the Bolsheviks. There is a wealth of detail in the story but not so much as would detract us from the enjoyment of the story. Espionage, counter-espionage, the ace of spies himself, double-agents, double-crossers...all these flit across the pages in a realistic and exciting way. All the characters are extremely well-drawn and Mr Growick, most importantly, does not falter with a very good ear for Holmesian dialogue indeed. Highly recommended. A five-star effort."
The Baker Street Society

www.mxpublishing.com

Also From MX Publishing

London, 1920: Boston-bred Enoch Hale, working as a reporter for the Central News Syndicate, arrives on the scene shortly after a music hall escape artist is found hanging from the ceiling in his dressing room. What at first appears to be a suicide turns out to be murder.

The second in the Enoch Hale series –
'The Poisoned Penman'.

www.mxpublishing.com